Maxwell feared the worst— he was too late

Ward pulled him aside and explained the situation. "They made their routine check with us, and that's it. No way to raise them now. They're in position and ready."

"Recall them," Maxwell insisted.

Ward looked at the CIA man. "Can't. Even if we had radio contact we couldn't just recall them. No authorization."

"I'll get you authorization," said Maxwell.

"Radio contact must be initiated at their end. The men in the field, because of the changing nature of their situation, control the radio."

"But they've been compromised," said Maxwell.

"Sir," said Ward, "I'm sorry as hell, but there's nothing I can do about it."

Maxwell took a deep breath. "I'm talking about fellow Green Berets."

"I understand that."

Maxwell stood there, feeling like his world was coming to an end. It began to look as if he might be throwing away his career. But then, maybe he deserved it because he had betrayed his friends.

VIETNAM: GROUND ZERO.™

PUPPET SOLDIERS

ERIC HELM

A GOLD EAGLE BOOK FROM
WORLDWIDE.

TORONTO · NEW YORK · LONDON · PARIS
AMSTERDAM · STOCKHOLM · HAMBURG
ATHENS · MILAN · TOKYO · SYDNEY

First edition December 1989

ISBN 0-373-62721-1

VIETNAM: GROUND ZERO ™

PUPPET SOLDIERS

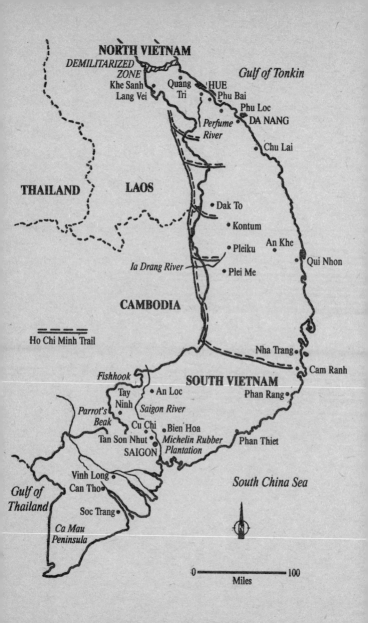

PROLOGUE

The tiny outpost, hidden in the thick jungle only a few miles
from the border with South Vietnam, baked under the late-
afternoon sun. The huts were little more than mud and
thatch, offering almost no protection from the heat or mon-
soon rains. Two huts—the radio shack and the headquarters
of General Kong Samphan—had extra protection around the
bottom to deflect shrapnel. But the protective barrier
wouldn't defeat a well-aimed rifle bullet.

The cooking shack had a layered chimney system designed to disperse smoke so that American pilots violating
the neutrality of Cambodia wouldn't be able to spot the camp
from the air. The sleeping quarters for the soldiers were
constructed of wooden platforms elevated a few feet above
the jungle floor, and partial walls to allow circulation of the
breeze.

Kong Samphan, the only Cambodian officer in the outpost, stood in the doorway of his hut and watched the approaching North Vietnamese soldiers. For two days his
scouts had reported the soldiers' progress as they walked

along the Ho Chi Minh Trail, then diverted westward toward his camp. He had known they were coming because they had requested the meeting with him months earlier.

Samphan was a middle-aged man, approaching his fiftieth birthday. He was small, with dark skin that looked almost black sometimes. His black hair was streaked with gray and his round face featured the characteristics of a fat person, though he wasn't fat. He had dark brown eyes and a neatly trimmed mustache.

Unlike the majority of his soldiers, he wore a tailored uniform, purchased in Hong Kong and sewn together in a single day. One of twelve that he owned, it was dark green with light green piping. The berrylike clusters sewn to the collar indicated that he was a general, and although the official Cambodian government hadn't confirmed the rank, the North Vietnamese who were coming to visit, fully approved of his self-promotion.

Although his men were armed with a variety of weapons, many of them taken from the bodies of dead South Vietnamese soldiers, Samphan wore a Soviet-made Tokarev TT-33 pistol in a black holster of highly polished leather. It had been a gift from his North Vietnamese friends, along with a dozen brand-new AK-47s, which had been handed out to his most trusted NCOs.

The ten NVA soldiers looked tired after their trek from Hanoi. Their green uniforms were sweat-stained with salt rings under the arms and down the fronts. They had stubble on their chins. All wore packs and carried canteens and AKs. Two of them also sported pistols. That identified the officers for Samphan, although the men wore no other insignia.

One of the officers walked up to where Samphan stood, took off his pith helmet with the red star centered on it and wiped the sweat from his face. He looked up at Samphan. "Are we on time, Comrade General?"

Samphan ignored the question. "Who are you?"

"I am Colonel Phan Dinh Khai of the People's Army of Vietnam with greetings from your friends in Hanoi." He bowed slightly as he spoke.

Two Cambodian NCOs appeared next to the North Vietnamese soldiers. Samphan waved at them and ordered, "See that our friends receive food and water while I confer with the officers."

Khai turned and barked an order in Vietnamese. The men fell out to follow the two NCOs. The second officer separated himself from the group and walked forward, standing next to the colonel. Samphan noticed that he was taller than the colonel and that his skin was lighter colored. Also, his uniform was ill-fitting, as if it had been taken from a supply shed only a few days earlier. These things didn't escape Samphan's scrutiny, but he said nothing about them. Instead he took a step backward, bowed and indicated the doorway. "Please make my quarters your home, humble as they are."

Khai climbed onto the notched log that functioned as steps and entered the headquarters hut. Inside was a rough table made from scrap wood, some of it obviously stolen from the Americans in South Vietnam judging from the stenciling on it. There were four chairs, also homemade, a small field desk in one corner and a picture of a naked blonde ripped from *Playboy*, hanging on the wall opposite the door so that visitors would see it the moment they entered.

The floor, made of split logs, was dirty and uneven. The walls were thatched, as was the roof. There was a lizard clutching one of the wooden support poles, head down, as if it were about to flee something hidden in the thatch of the roof above it.

"We have few comforts here," said Sampham.

"That will change for the better soon," said Khai. "When the American imperialists are driven from South Vietnam and their puppet soldiers are exterminated, life will be better for all our people."

Samphan nodded knowingly and then pointed at the chairs. "Be seated, gentlemen. I can only offer you some water for your thirst and roast monkey for your hunger. It's the very best we have here."

"You're too kind, Comrade General," said Khai. "Your sacrifice will be rewarded when the imperialists are gone and the land is returned to the people."

Samphan walked to the door and ordered the food and drink, then returned to sit at the table. He stared at the two men across from him and thought of his family, living in squalor in Phnom Penh. His wife seemed to be sick all the time and his four children cried because there was never enough to eat. He thought of their dirty room, which was filled with terrible odors and masses of insects. The reward the North Vietnamese offered would take his family out of that dirty room. It would put food on his table and provide medicine for his wife. It would do all the things the government was supposed to do, had promised to do, but didn't.

"Comrade General," said Khai, "we're here to negotiate the use of your lands west of the border. We'll pay you for their use, reward your men for their assistance to us, and we'll assure that your family, and the families of your men, are safe from reprisals by either your government or the American imperialists in South Vietnam."

"And for this, I must do . . . what?"

"Nothing, except refuse to allow the Americans to cross the border. Fight the Americans when necessary, keeping them in South Vietnam, and issue protests to the world press about American violations of neutrality."

"I have no access to the world press," said Samphan quietly, almost sadly.

"We'll assist you in that matter, as well," said Khai, gesturing broadly. "We'll bring a journalist with us next time. He'll instruct you in the use of the press, provide assistance in gaining access to the news media and prepare documents for release."

Samphan nodded his understanding.

"You must deny, however, that we've met. You must always deny you have had any contact with us or our representatives. The people of Vietnam respect the sovereignty of the Cambodian nation and the right of the Cambodian people to exist."

"Of course."

Khai glanced at the man who was with him, the other North Vietnamese officer who was sitting quietly, watching the proceedings. "Do you have anything to add, Comrade?"

"Nothing."

"Then we should eat," said Khai. "And drink a toast to the cooperation of our two nations in the fight against the American aggressors." He waved a hand at the door as if summoning waiters to bring in the food and drink Samphan had ordered.

Samphan looked at the Vietnamese envoys and wondered what had happened. Somehow they had taken charge of the meeting, dictating terms to him and then declaring the meeting over by calling for the food and drink he had ordered for them. He'd have to be more careful, or he'd find himself on the outside looking in again. He'd have to be very careful.

1

MACV HEADQUARTERS
SAIGON, RVN

Jerry Maxwell was sweating profusely as he sat at his desk in the bowels of the MACV building. Even with the air conditioner blowing a stream of cold air at him, the moisture continued to trickle down his body. He wasn't that hot, but he was nervous, worried by the information he had received and afraid of the reaction of various officials, both military and civilian, to that material. On paper it didn't look very good, and voiced to a briefing of a dozen or so leaders, it would sound even worse.

Maxwell was a short, skinny man who didn't tan in the tropical sun. He burned and peeled and then started the process over again. His black hair, now sweat-damp, hung down over his forehead. He'd been in Vietnam for more than a year now, and had taken on a gaunt look, his eyes ringed in black, giving his head the appearance of a skull. For a CIA operative it was an appropriate look.

Maxwell was dressed in his standard uniform of white suit, white shirt and narrow black tie. He had opened his collar and loosened his tie. His suit jacket was hung over the back of his chair and there were sweat stains under his arms. He'd turned up the air conditioner once, but it hadn't done any good. He was still miserable.

Rocking back in his chair, he picked up the Coke can from the left side of his desk and shook it once. Naturally it was empty. He couldn't understand how every time he wanted a drink of Coke, the can was empty. He'd buy them in the morning, and before he could reach his office, they'd be empty. He'd troop upstairs, signing out at the control point, buy another and in minutes would find himself wanting more but the can would again be empty. There never seemed to be a chance to enjoy them.

Maxwell's office was tucked away in a corner of the building, out of easy access to everyone. To get to it, an officer or enlisted man needed to have security clearance and then have his name on an access roster. Visitors were sometimes required to wait until Maxwell came and got them.

Because it was out of the way and hard to get to, and because Maxwell wasn't considered one of the influential civilians in Vietnam, his office had none of the luxuries. There were cinder-block walls painted light green, four filing cabinets, one of which was massive and had a combination lock. His dilapidated battleship-gray desk was shoved into a corner. The bottom drawer stuck. A line of empty Coke cans were arrayed against a wall on the edge of his desk.

The visitor's chair, sitting next to the desk, was made of vinyl and patched with black electrician's tape in half a dozen spots. On the wall was a single picture—a framed Army lithograph of the Wagon Box Fight.

Even though Maxwell was stuck in an out-of-the-way corner and his office wasn't as opulent as those of the generals and higher-ranking civilians, his function as a control officer for some of the Special Forces missions, and his relationship with certain members of the Special Forces, gave him a power that few other men in South Vietnam had. It was little enough compensation for all his work.

Glancing at his watch, Maxwell realized it was almost time for the briefing. He turned to the raw data again and read through the agent's report. Everyone knew the NVA had been operating in Cambodia since the beginning of the war, but now their activities had taken on a new dimension.

Using a pen and a legal pad, Maxwell made some notes, circled a couple of paragraphs and numbered them so that he would be able to refer to them during his briefing. He stood and checked the office quickly, making sure all classified material was picked up and put into the safe. He stepped to the safe, pushed each of the drawers closed, locked them and then jerked on the doors to make sure they were locked.

Finally he stuffed the report into a folder marked secret on the top, bottom and back. Putting the folder into a leather case, he yanked on his coat from the rear of his chair.

Sighing, he gave the office a final glance, afraid he'd left something out. In the past week two majors and a sergeant had been disciplined for leaving classified data unguarded. There hadn't been a breach of security—nothing had been compromised—but everyone with access to classified material was being watched closely.

Shrugging into his coat, he moved to the door and opened it. As he stepped out into the hallway, which looked more like a tunnel leading to a medieval dungeon than a staircase leading to the first floor, he pulled the door shut, listening for the click that ensured it was locked. Satisfied, he walked down the corridor.

An MP stood guard at the iron gate. He held an M-16 and wore a holstered .45 on his hip. Without acknowledging the man, Maxwell signed out, then walked up the stairs and entered another hallway. Here, the floor was tiled in green and the walls were painted in the same pale green as his office.

Pictures and posters on the walls helped to relieve the monotony of the sickly paint. The pictures showed the various military chains of command and the posters were all designed to remind soldiers to wear their uniforms properly, to safeguard COMSEC and to stay away from Vietnamese women.

Ignoring the offices on both sides of the corridor, most of them staffed by young men in jungle fatigues, Maxwell walked down to the other end of the building. The textures changed as he approached the area where the highest-ranking officers were housed. The green tile gave way to carpeting, and the color of the paint changed from sickly green-yellow to a richer, more verdant shade. The doors changed from unstained pine to rich mahogany. These doors were closed, and there were small brass plaques on them, announcing the functions of the offices hidden behind.

Maxwell reached the conference room and stopped outside the door. He glanced down the corridor at the people scurrying about—men in jungle fatigues and khakis, carrying notebooks and folders, looking as if they should belong to a corporation whose uniforms were gray flannel suits, and who should be worrying about production quotas and shipping schedules. Somehow it didn't look like the headquarters of a combat organization conducting a war.

Taking a deep breath, he opened the door and stepped inside. There were a half-dozen men standing around, waiting. Four of them wore starched jungle fatigues. Everything about the uniforms was perfect, right down to the sleeves, which were rolled halfway between elbows and shoulders, just as regulations dictated. There wasn't a wrinkle, crease or stray thread on any of the bright green uniforms. All of them looked as if they had been issued that morning.

The other two men wore khakis. Again they were immaculate. The rows of ribbons above the left breast pocket were aligned perfectly. Both men wore jump wings and both had colonel's eagles glittering on their collars.

Maxwell didn't recognize any of the men in the room, but that wasn't unusual. Since he normally worked with the Special Forces, he didn't mingle with the regular Army troops very often, except to brief them and their superiors.

One of the khaki-clad officers glanced at Maxwell. "You the Central Intelligence guy?"

"Yes."

"Burt, let the general know we're all here now."

One of the men in fatigues nodded. "Yes, sir."

A moment later the general appeared in the door. A new man, wearing fatigues and the gold bars of a second lieutenant, announced, "Gentlemen, General Hansen."

The military men came to attention as Hansen swept into the room, his aides and a couple of NCOs trailing. He was a small, thin man with jet-black hair slicked down. The skin of his face was deeply tanned, and it looked as if he had shaved sometime in the past hour or so. He wore a khaki uniform, but not with the precision of the colonels. His was wrinkled, and there were sweat stains under the arms and down the front. He wore a single row of ribbons, all of them combat decorations instead of meritorious service awards.

As he dropped into a chair at the head of the table, he said, "Gentlemen, please be seated and we'll get this show on the road."

Maxwell wiped the sweat from his face and sat down. He noticed that the air-conditioning wasn't as effective on the ground floor as it was below in his office. The sun heated the building, making the air conditioner work harder.

He opened his folder and waited for General Hansen to call on him, dreading the moment he'd have to start the intel portion of the briefing.

SPECIAL FORCES CAPTAIN MacKenzie K. Gerber crouched
in the steam-bath heat of the jungle, peering through a gap
in the trees and bushes. The object of his attention was a
farmer plowing a field. The man walked behind a water buffalo, a long, thin switch in one hand, which he occasionally
flicked at the animal's hindquarters. Gerber had been there
since before dawn, along with a squad of highly trained men,
watching the trails and roads that meandered through the
area. They were searching for signs of an enemy buildup in
the region, and they had yet to see anything that suggested
the VC or the NVA even knew the place existed.

Gerber's face was painted in a nightmarish mask of greens,
blacks and grays. He hadn't moved since the sun had come
up. Now he leaned back against the rough bark of a palm
tree, his rifle in his right hand. Sweat formed and dripped,
running down the side of his face, tickling his back and
soaking his jungle fatigues around the waist where he wore
a pistol belt holding a first-aid kit, three canteens and other
equipment.

As the farmer turned and started back in the knee-deep
water of the rice paddy, Gerber realized nothing was going
to happen. During the night, after they had gotten into position, there had been no movement. They'd heard the
sounds of music drifting on the light breeze, Vietnamese
music played on a small battery-powered radio and broadcast from Saigon. There had been voices for a while, but
those had faded until the only noise had been the radio, the
quiet buzz of insects and the ever-present pop of distant artillery, sounding like the thunder of an approaching storm.

The night had passed with nothing of interest happening.
At dawn the people of the nearby village had begun to stir,
coming out to light cooking fires or to make sure a stray round
hadn't killed an ox or water buffalo sometime during the
night. There was nothing in the actions of the people that

suggested there was anything wrong. The village appeared to be peaceful and full of people trying to avoid contact with the war.

Figuring that the VC or NVA, if they were around, would be appearing soon, Gerber and his men didn't move. They ignored the feelings of hunger and thirst and sat perfectly still in the growing heat of the tropical morning.

Around them the jungle came alive. Monkeys screamed at one another. Birds squawked, launched themselves into the sky, wheeled around and dived for cover among the thick palm leaves and branches of the hardwood trees. Lizards scrambled through the thick, rotting carpet of the jungle floor. Insects buzzed around the eyes of the captain and his men, darting in to taste the salt of sweat.

Throughout the morning Gerber watched the Vietnamese go about their daily lives. Farmers marched off to the fields to tend the rice. Some of the women went with them. Others stayed behind, squatting in the little shade and working with stone tools. The radio that had been turned on all night still played music, but now it was louder.

Overhead they heard American helicopters, sometimes a single ship at three or four thousand feet, sometimes a flight of ten or more, flying at fifteen hundred feet. The soldiers riding in the back, all armed with M-16s, M-79s and shotguns, were easily visible.

A shadow flickered to the left, and Master Sergeant Anthony B. Fetterman leaned close. "Time to go, Captain?"

Slowly Gerber turned to face the other man. Fetterman was a small, almost diminutive man who, despite appearances, was exceptionally strong. His balding head was hidden under a camou-striped boonie hat that was pulled low over his eyes. Like Gerber, he had painted his face to blend into the greens, grays and blacks of the jungle. His heavy beard, which required him to shave twice a day, added to the hideous pattern on his skin.

"Time to go," agreed Gerber. He rocked back and sat down on the moist ground. Pulling out his canteen, he took a drink and let the warm water trickle down his throat. Finally he capped the canteen. "Give the men ten minutes to eat, drink and relieve themselves. Then we'll be on the move to the southeast."

"Yes, sir."

As Fetterman disappeared into the moisture-laden foliage, Gerber turned and looked to the right, where he saw more jungle, with sunlight lancing downward in shafts visible against the darkness of the trees and bushes. Suddenly there was a flicker as a brightly colored bird dropped from a branch, snagged a lizard and then flapped back up into the trees, disappearing.

Gerber touched his forehead with the sleeve of his jungle fatigues, leaving a ragged sweat stain there. He checked his watch and wondered if it wasn't time to pull the whole patrol out of the field. They'd had no luck in three days.

THE WEATHER IN SAIGON was almost as oppressive as it was in the jungle. The difference was that the verdant growth in the field absorbed the heat while the brick, stone and concrete in the city radiated it back, making it seem ten or fifteen degrees hotter.

Robin Morrow stood at the window in front of the city room and fanned herself with a file folder, wondering why the air-conditioning always seemed to break down on the hottest days. Opening the windows did no good as the odors and noises of Saigon drifted up from the streets, adding to the misery without cooling the interior. The din of traffic, of people, of bars clamoring for patrons, did no good, either. It got on her nerves and reminded her of where she was—in the foulest, most disgusting city in the free world. In a pit. In the darkest reaches of hell where the promise of a transfer to the Sahara seemed to be more appealing.

Morrow was a tall, slender woman whose brown hair had been bleached blond by her time in-country. She had fine features and her tanned skin accentuated her green eyes. She had pulled her shoulder-length hair back and used a rubber band to fashion a ponytail, trying to keep cool. She wore her standard working uniform of khaki jumpsuit with the sleeves and the legs cut off, which was also a failed attempt to keep cool.

Mark Hodges, one of the senior editors, approached her from the rear. He had been interested in her from the moment she'd set foot in the city room, but he'd never done more than make heavily veiled suggestions that they go to dinner. She'd never seemed interested in that, so he never really asked her for a date.

Hodges was typical of the journalists in Vietnam. He hated the heat and sun and found excuses not to go into the field. He was one of the few people who had managed to put on weight while in Vietnam. It was because he tried not to go outside, and tried to have long, large lunches and leisurely dinners in what had once been the four-star hotels in Saigon.

Hodges had thick black hair that he greased in the morning and then didn't bother combing the rest of the day. He was a heavy-featured man who was rapidly going to fat. He had given up wearing suits and now wore khaki safari clothes, though he hadn't bothered to find the large-caliber bullets to stuff through the loops on the jacket.

He stopped next to Morrow but didn't look at her. "Smells bad out there."

"Always smells bad," said Morrow. "Heat traps the odors close to the ground and there's never a breeze to blow it away. It sort of festers down there."

"Smells like shit."

Morrow glanced at him in disbelief. Hodges had been in Vietnam for nearly two years and still didn't know about the open sewer system. Raw sewage was dumped into the river, and there were stagnant pools of it in many of the poorer residential areas. It was an odor that pervaded the city and stayed there, hanging in the stagnant air.

The war didn't help. Every time someone tried to build a sewer system or a treatment facility, the VC blew it up. Almost everyone felt it was more important to build schools and hospitals, and so the sewage problem compounded itself with the arrival of the refugees who streamed into Saigon daily.

"Smells worse than that on the street. Especially now that we've helped create a smog problem," Morrow observed.

Hodges pulled a white handkerchief from his pocket and mopped his face. As he stuffed it back out of sight, he said, "I wish it would rain."

"Why? That'll just make it worse." She turned from the window and looked at the city room. There were rows of desks, most of them military surplus. They were gray metal behemoths, scarred by years of service in Vietnam. On many of them sat old manual typewriters because the power was so intermittent that electric ones were often no better than expensive paperweights.

To one side were glass offices, most of them assigned to the editors, though the senior correspondents had two that they shared. Along the back wall, near the doors, were several filing cabinets that held information about Saigon, about Vietnam and about the war. Opposite the glass offices, on the other side of the room, was another bank of windows. They looked out onto a worse section of Saigon.

Morrow leaned back against the windowsill and wiped the sweat from her face. She was soaking wet. Her hair hung down and her jumpsuit looked as if it had just been washed. Beads of sweat dripped from her nose and chin and ran down her neck.

"You know," she said, "I'm beginning to really hate this place. More and more each day. More each time something goes wrong, like the failure of the air-conditioning or another power outage."

"How long you been here?"

Morrow, as a joke, looked at her watch. "Eighteen months."

"With time off in Japan."

"You think I didn't deserve that time in Japan? You think I was skating there?"

"No, not at all. You know, duty in Vietnam is strictly voluntary. You want to go home and find another assignment, I'm sure it can be arranged."

Until that moment Morrow hadn't thought about it. She had almost believed that she was stuck in Vietnam, just as the soldiers were. They knew they could go home at the end of the year, but Morrow didn't know that. She was stuck in Saigon as long as the newspaper wanted her there, or until something happened so that she had to return. There was no preplanned date for her return to the States.

As she thought about it, she realized that could be the reason she had been so depressed the past few weeks. The war seemed to stretch out in front of her like the endless tracks of a railroad. She couldn't see the end of it. She would be there forever, no matter what the military and Administration told the people in the World.

"How soon?" she asked suddenly.

"How soon what?"

"How soon can I get out of here? How soon before I can go home?"

"You sure that's what you want?"

Morrow shrugged. "I don't know." Again she wiped at the sweat, but her hand was so wet that it didn't do any good.

Hodges folded his arms across his chest. "I could probably have a replacement here in a couple of days. Maybe move someone up to your beat and request someone from the pool in the States. Would you want to stick around long enough to help train the man? Introduce him to your sources?"

"Mark, you're moving awfully fast. I say that I'm a little depressed and you're ready to move me out."

"I don't want people working here who are unhappy. If you don't like your work, you do a shitty job."

"I saw you give David a bottle and send him out to get drunk and laid."

"That what you need?"

Morrow grinned. "I don't know. Maybe."

"Where's that Green Beret captain friend of yours?"

Morrow twisted and pointed west. "Out there somewhere crushing communism and saving the free world for the greater good of the human race."

"Robin," said Hodges seriously, "maybe it *is* time you went home for a year or two and covered stories that don't threaten your life."

"Okay," she said suddenly. "Why don't you just get on the phone or whatever you have to do and see about getting me the hell out of here?"

"You serious?"

For an instant she didn't say a word. It was as if she were considering the question. Finally she nodded. "Yes, I'm quite serious."

"Then we'll get on it."

"Thanks."

2

**MACV HEADQUARTERS
SAIGON**

General Hansen had spent the first few minutes of the meeting reviewing what he had learned earlier when he'd met with members of General Westmoreland's staff. Hansen sat at the head of the table, the leather folder open in front of him, reading from his notes. He found that none of the information was very interesting. It was just routine stuff that concerned logistics but not the conduct of the war.

Hansen finally flipped the folder closed and stared at Maxwell. "What do you have for us?"

The CIA man slowly got to his feet. He wiped the sweat from his face and opened his own folder. Leaning forward, palms flat on the table, he studied the documents between his hands as if he'd never seen them before.

"Mr. Maxwell?"

Glancing up, Maxwell, said, "Yes, General. Before I start I want to point out that anything said in this room is classified as secret and must not be discussed in environments where security can't be guaranteed. And I should also make it clear that we're dealing with raw data here. I haven't had

a chance to evaluate or confirm it, but it's important enough
to discuss."

"Understood, Mr. Maxwell," said Hansen.

"Then with that out of the way," said Maxwell, "I'll begin." He turned toward a map on an easel and walked over
to it. Using his middle finger, he pointed to the region known
as the Parrot's Beak.

"Here, well inside Cambodia, safe from American artillery, helicopters and air strikes, are various sanctuaries used
by both the North Vietnamese and Vietcong."

"Yes, yes," said Hansen impatiently, waving his hand to
make Maxwell speak faster.

"Because of various international laws and agreements,
and not wanting to risk a challenge by the Cambodian government or direct intervention by the Chinese, we've allowed this situation to exist."

"Is there a point to this?" asked Hansen.

"Sorry, General," said Maxwell, "but I wanted the background of the situation understood by everyone in this room.
I want everyone to know that the situation, the North Vietnamese in Cambodia, is an ongoing problem that didn't arise
in the past few weeks. I want everyone to know that some sort
of agreement, though not formal, has existed between the
lawful government in Phnom Penh and Hanoi."

"We understand that."

"Fine." Maxwell returned to the table and sorted through
the documents in his folder. "We have now received word
that certain Cambodian leaders sympathetic to the North
Vietnamese cause are slowly being elevated into positions of
power. North Vietnamese representatives are meeting with
these Cambodians. In exchange for cooperation in con-
structing bases in Cambodia, the North Vietnamese are
lending political support so that these Cambodian leaders

will become more active in opposing U.S. policies in Southeast Asia."

"Meaning what?" asked Hansen.

"The North Vietnamese are slowly maneuvering to take out the current power structure and replace it with one of their own design. They'll slowly eliminate, through assassination and abduction, the rulers of Cambodia who don't cooperate, actions that will effectively knock out the existing government."

Hansen sat quietly for a moment and then tented his fingers under his chin as if in deep thought. "Why is this a sudden concern to you and your people?"

Maxwell sat down and shook his head. This wasn't the reaction he had expected. He'd thought everyone would be angry. They'd want men in the field immediately. They'd want to know how the North Vietnamese had been able to infiltrate the Cambodian power structure. He hadn't expected to be asked why it was a concern.

"The concern," said Maxwell, speaking slowly, "is that thousands of North Vietnamese troops will be stationed in Cambodia. Now there are token bases and supply depots, but the majority of the manpower and equipment is shipped from the North and merely transits Cambodia. If they could use Cambodia as a staging area, then major supply line problems would be eliminated. But, more importantly, if Cambodia suddenly swung into the North Vietnamese camp, they could tap a manpower pool of several million military-age males."

"Uh-huh," said Hansen.

Maxwell looked up at the general. Obviously the man didn't understand the implications. Maxwell sat quietly for a moment and then tried to explain the situation.

"Politically, Cambodia is neutral. Theoretically the North Vietnamese can't operate inside the Cambodian borders.

That limits the assistance they receive from the Cambodians, and because of that it helps our cause in the South. If that suddenly changed, all our bases, camps and outposts near the border, within artillery range, would be in jeopardy. The course of the war would change dramatically.''

''All right,'' said Hansen. ''I'll accept your assessment that the situation is bad. What do you intend to do about it?''

Again Maxwell was unprepared. He had only wanted to offer the information. It was up to the generals and top civilian leaders, in consultation with the South Vietnamese, to decide on a course of action. He handed out the intelligence and others made decisions based on it.

Without thinking, he blurted, ''We should eliminate the problem and kill the Cambodian leaders.''

He suddenly wished he could bite his tongue. He wished he'd said nothing. Now it was too late.

But Hansen merely nodded. ''We'll take it under advisement. Anything else?''

Maxwell rocked back in his chair. He sighed, then said, ''That's it.'' He couldn't believe they were through with him. He'd thought someone would point out that the intelligence should have been uncovered earlier, that fingers would be pointed at him for not doing his job well. It was as if he'd told them that the North Vietnamese lived in Hanoi. No one was surprised or concerned. If they didn't care, neither did he.

FETTERMAN STOPPED, pointed right and left, then told the strikers where to take up positions. Satisfied the men were alert and waiting, he slipped to the rear where Gerber crouched. Leaning close, he whispered, ''Someone off to the right. Moving with us.''

''Farmer?''

"Doubtful. Moves when we move and stops when we stop. I'd say ten, twelve guys who know what they're doing."

"How long they been there?"

"Twenty minutes."

Gerber nodded.

"I think," said Fetterman, "that you should break off here, circle around to the left, away from them, and then come back to the trail and set up for an ambush."

"I'd have to take the majority of the men," said Gerber. "That leaves you with four or five."

"Four would be plenty. They're not going to hit us yet."

Gerber pulled the camouflage cover from the face of his watch and glanced at the time. He knew exactly what Fetterman meant. Charlie didn't attack during the day when the Americans could see what was going on. The VC liked to hit units as they were pulling out of the field at the end of the day. It meant they were reluctant to redeploy because they were tired from a day of humping the boonies, and with night coming on, support from the various aviation assets, both Army and Air Force, was limited. Charlie held the cards. "Why don't you hold here, eat lunch, relax and then move out in about an hour? We'll slip off now and get into position."

"Yes, sir."

"Anyone special you want?"

"Tyson would be nice. Any three of the striker NCOs."

Gerber wiped his face again and glanced up at the jungle canopy. "One hour from now."

"Yes, sir."

Gerber got up and slipped to the rear. He tapped Tyson on the shoulder and leaned close to his ear. "You're on Fetterman. Move on up."

Without a word, Tyson did as he was told. He was a big, young man on his first tour in Vietnam. Gerber hadn't worked with him prior to this mission, but the man had made it through the various schools at Fort Bragg and Camp McKall, so the captain had confidence in him.

He approached Sergeant Thai and crouched near him. Thai was a Vietnamese soldier who had spent ten years fighting various enemies, including the Viet Minh and then the Vietcong. He was a middle-aged man with a series of scars on his face, the result of a rocket attack two years earlier. Missing two fingers on his left hand, he was thin, short and filled with hate.

Gerber whispered, "I want you to select two other men, men you trust, and then report to Sergeant Fetterman."

"Yes, Captain."

Gerber found the last of the American Special Forces men on the patrol—Sergeant David Braver. Like Tyson, Braver was young, no more than twenty-one. He had finished high school, joined the Army and then gone right into the Special Forces. The rules had once kept first-termers out, but the meat grinder that was the Vietnam War made it impossible to fulfill manpower requirements.

"You're on me," said Gerber.

"Yes, sir."

Together they moved along the line of men, getting them on their feet. Gerber motioned them to be quiet. Now it was important that they slip through the jungle. No rattling equipment. No talking. No smoking. They had to move in silence so that the enemy had no idea they were on the move.

Gerber pointed at the men, telling them their positions in the formation. Then, looking at his compass, he began to move at a ninety-degree angle to the original line of march, away from where he suspected the enemy was hiding.

Slowly he moved through the jungle, stepping over rotting logs, walking around the thick trunks of hardwood trees and dodging the lacy, delicate branches of ferns. He avoided the thickest of the undergrowth, pushing aside the branches of some bushes with his rifle.

Stopping once, Gerber glanced over his shoulder and saw that the men were strung out behind him, following the path he'd made. He moved on until he came to the bank of a narrow, shallow stream, which he stepped across.

When he got to the other side, he halted and fell to one knee on the moist carpet of rotting vegetation. Without a command the men did the same, waiting for his next move. Gerber listened but heard nothing to indicate that the enemy was behind him, or that they had attacked Fetterman's tiny band.

Again he was up and moving, stepping carefully, toe out, rolling his foot down as he searched for booby traps in the jungle. The men with him surveyed the jungle around them, heads and shoulders swiveling as they tried to spot signs of an ambush. They moved slowly, trying to make no sound.

Before they had covered more than half a klick, Gerber was bathed in sweat. It soaked his hair and dripped down his face. It turned his jungle jacket black and stained the thick pistol belt around his waist. It made his skin itch, and he could feel it tickling his sides. Walking through the jungle was like walking through a steam bath, but it wasn't as pleasant. Here there was dirt, foul odors, noises from jungle animals and the constant threat of sudden death.

Gerber stopped again, checked his compass, then turned north, paralleling the path Fetterman would follow. Now he and his men should be a klick or more from the enemy soldiers, too far for them to hear a snapping twig or a muffled cry. They could relax slightly and pick up the pace.

Gerber didn't give them a chance to rest. They turned and hurried on, bypassing a huge hole with water in the bottom, the result of an errant bomb. As they skirted the edge of the crater, Gerber saw signs that indicated someone had bathed in the murky water, but there was no way of telling whether it was an American patrol, a Vietnamese family or enemy soldiers.

They hurried around the crater and dived back into the thick jungle. Gerber felt the thorns of a wait-a-minute vine rip his uniform and rucksack. Rather than jerk free, he twisted around and tried to pull the vine off. Failing, he used his knife to cut it.

After thirty minutes, Gerber called a halt. He pulled out his map and checked the terrain. Deep in the jungle there wasn't much in the way of landmarks—outcropping of rocks, slopes, valleys and streams. Sometimes there was a road, or hamlet or an American camp that told him where he was. Here there wasn't much of anything.

Using the compass as a guide, he turned back toward the path that Fetterman would be following. He got the men moving again, keeping them quiet. Gerber and his men now moved with exaggerated caution, not wanting to leave any sign, afraid it would tip off the enemy as they approached the trap.

After they had marched half a klick, Gerber was sure they were back to the original line of march. He spread everyone out, using Braver to anchor one end of the L-shaped ambush. As he positioned the men, he told each of them not to fire until he did. The signal to spring the ambush would be the detonation of a hand grenade. Once it exploded, they were to kill every enemy soldier.

Satisfied that the men were ready and that there was nothing more he could tell them, Gerber settled into his position next to the smooth trunk of a teak tree. The heavy roots, sticking up through the wet soil of the jungle floor, would offer some protection from the enemy if needed.

Overhead, the birds that had fallen silent as Gerber and his men had moved into the area began to sing again. At first there was only a single bird, almost as if it were announcing an end to the danger. Then another began and another until the upper canopy was alive with noise.

The monkeys were next, scampering through the canopy, hidden from the ground by the thick layer of interlocking branches and giant leaves. They rattled the trees as they leaped from one branch to another, flipping themselves up and scrambling on.

The screams of the animals were punctuated by the dripping of water, natural sounds that would mask the approach of an enemy as well as cover the noise Gerber and his strikers might make as they waited in ambush. Gerber glanced up, saw a flash of bright color and heard the squawk of one of the birds. Then he turned his attention back to the trail, where Fetterman and the enemy would be in a few minutes.

WHEN THE SHADOW FELL across her desk, Morrow looked up. Hodges was standing there, a file folder in his hand. He looked unhappy, but then he always looked unhappy. Next to him was a young man, no more than twenty-three or twenty-four with flyaway blond hair, pasty white skin and a sunburned nose. He was thin and looked uncomfortable in khaki clothes. A 35 mm camera hung around his neck.

"This is Jason Danforth," said Hodges. "He arrived this morning and has been assigned to our office."

"You move fast."

Hodges shrugged. "Would you believe an amazing coincidence?"

Morrow dropped her pencil onto the desk and shook her head. "I think you knew someone was coming and I just provided a simple out for a dilemma you saw brewing."

Hodges parked a haunch on her desk, letting his left foot dangle. "I knew someone was on the way, but there was no problem. There's enough work around here." He opened the folder. "Young Danforth is fresh out of school. Took a couple of months off to see the States, did some work for his father's paper and then got a job with us."

"Uh-huh," said Morrow noncommittally.

"Got good credentials," added Hodges.

"Fresh out of school and hits a gravy assignment," said Morrow. "A career can be made here. One good story, one shining report and the reporter can write his or her ticket. Reporters fighting to get to Vietnam because it's a choice assignment now. This is where the news is and it means the opportunity for a nightly slot on the network. Recognition."

"Exactly," said Hodges. "I want you to show Danforth the ropes here, introduce him around and see that he learns where to go to develop sources."

"Thanks a bunch," said Morrow.

Hodges stood and waved his folder at his glass cube. "I'll be in my office if you have any questions." Then, rather than wait for questions, he beat a hasty retreat.

Morrow hung her head and studied the notes in front of her, almost as if she were unaware of Danforth. Finally she looked up at him. "Who do you know?"

"Ma'am?"

"Oh, Christ," snapped Morrow. "My name's Robin."

Grinning, he said, "Okay, Robin."

"Now, who do you know?"

Danforth shrugged. "My father arranged this. Thought it would be good for me. See some of the world. See how the other half lives."

"Or dies. Your father has some strange ideas. You could get killed here."

"He did point out that I could get killed walking down the street at home and that as a journalist here I was as safe as a reporter in New York City."

"Grab a seat," said Morrow, "and tell me about your-self."

Danforth dragged a chair over and pushed it close to the front of Morrow's desk. As he sat down, he leaned forward, elbows on the desk. He lowered his voice. "I'm glad to be here, in Saigon, where I can see what's really going on."

"What's really going on?" said Morrow. "What do you mean? What's really going on?"

"Well, I think it's obvious from everything I've seen and read that there is a big cover-up going on. The military is lying to the American people. The South Vietnamese gov-ernment is lying to us and to its own people."

"Sure," said Morrow. She suddenly felt like the old-timer about to retire, the one who'd seen it all, who'd done it all and who was now so cynical that she believed nothing she read and only half of what she saw. Now she was looking at a fresh-faced kid who knew the government was hiding in-formation, and he was just the man to find it. It made her feel so old, and she had just celebrated her twenty-ninth birth-day.

"I mean," he continued, "no one has told us what's really going on. Take Tet. We're told that nothing's happening, that the enemy's defeated. And the next thing, they're run-ning through the streets of Saigon."

"Where are they now?"

"What?"

Morrow pointed at the window. "Where's the enemy now?"

"I don't understand," said Danforth.

"Because you don't think things through. You blow in here after what, five hours in-country, and talk about lies and half-truths and misrepresentations, but you don't think things through. You don't see the enemy running through the streets of Saigon now, do you?"

"No, not now."

"Well, think about that. If the enemy was so successful, why didn't they hold on to their gains. Why aren't there enemy soldiers running through the streets today?"

"That's not important now," said Danforth. "What's important is letting the people know what's happening in the war."

"And that is?"

He sat up then and glanced over his shoulder at the windows. "We need to get out there and see what it is. Learn the real facts."

"Out in the field?" asked Morrow.

"Certainly. That's where we're going to learn the truth," said Danforth.

Afraid of the answer, Morrow hesitated to ask the question but knew she had to. That even if she didn't, he would tell her. Finally she asked, "And what's the truth?"

"The United States is engaging in an illegal war of imperialism. What else could it be?"

Morrow sighed. "Yeah, what else could it be?"

3

THE JUNGLE
NORTHWEST OF SAIGON
NEAR THE CAMBODIAN
BORDER

Fetterman moved through the jungle like an early-morning mist. He made no noise and didn't disturb the jungle floor. Those behind him, Tyson and the three strikers, didn't have Fetterman's ability, and it was those men whom Gerber heard shuffling quietly. It was nothing definite, just a quiet rustle of cloth against the leaves of a plant, or the snap of a stick lying on the ground. Unnatural noises that told Gerber Fetterman and his team were close.

The master sergeant appeared suddenly at the edge of the ambush zone like an apparition. He slipped along the trail, looking right and left, but not acknowledging the presence of the ambushers. Gerber knew Fetterman had spotted them, even though they were well hidden.

The patrol continued through the killing zone and walked on out. Fetterman didn't stop, but led his men deeper into the jungle. He was going to set up a blocking force in case some of the VC managed to avoid the trap and escape into the jungle.

Two hundred meters behind Fetterman's tiny patrol, the Vietcong followed. Gerber turned so that he was looking down the trail. At first there was nothing to see, but then a single man dressed in black pajamas appeared. He wore a khaki chest pouch that held three spare magazines. On his feet were Ho Chi Minh sandals made from truck tires. He carried an AK-47 and seemed to be concentrating on the ground in front of him, following the trail left by Fetterman's soldiers.

Five meters behind him, emerging from shadows, were two more enemy soldiers. Both were dressed like the first, carried AKs and wore chest pouches. Unlike the point man, they were searching the jungle on both sides of the trail, looking for booby traps and signs of an ambush.

With his eyes on the approaching enemy soldiers, Gerber slowly reached down for a grenade. With the index finger of his left hand, he pulled the pin free. It was simple to do because he had already straightened it slightly. Holding the safety spoon tightly, he cocked his arm back like an outfielder about to nail a base runner.

The point man advanced, coming even with the center of the ambush and then passing beyond it. He hesitated for a moment, his head cocked to one side as if listening, and then continued to move. More of the patrol appeared. They were dressed as Vietcong, but they seemed to be better disciplined than the average VC. Well-trained soldiers masquerading as VC.

Gerber spotted the end of the patrol. Seeing it, he rocked back and threw his grenade. There was a quiet rattling as the grenade sailed through the thin vegetation. One enemy soldier dropped to the ground and another fired a quick burst from his AK, as if the sudden noise had frightened him.

The grenade detonated with a shattering explosion that ripped apart the rear guard. There were screams and cries of fright and pain.

And then all of Gerber's strikers were firing, each man burning through his magazine as quickly as possible. The sustained firing continued until the sound of individual shots was lost.

On the trail the Vietcong danced and fell under the impact of the rounds. One man tried to return fire. He dropped to his knee, raised his AK and was hit by an M-16 round. He rolled backward, jerking the trigger as he fell, his rounds tearing into the canopy overhead.

And as quickly as it had started, it was all over. There had been no return fire from the VC. They had all gone down under the initial bursts, all wounded or dead. One man turned to flee and was lifted from his feet by a burst that sent him sprawling on the ground.

"Cease fire," ordered Gerber. "Cease fire."

Slowly, as the men finished the rounds in their magazines, the firing stopped. A deafening silence fell on the jungle. Smoke drifted on a light breeze, highlighting the shafts of sunlight that penetrated the canopy.

From the trail there were quiet groans from the dying men. Gerber stood up slowly, his M-16 pointed at the enemy on the ground. The air was heavy with the metallic odor of blood. There was a quiet buzzing as flies began to gather.

Cautiously Gerber came out of hiding. In front of him were the bodies of two VC soldiers. Blood saturated their uniforms and the ground under them. The face of one of them had been blown away, leaving a crimson mess on the gleaming white of his skull. The other had lost a hand and part of one leg. There were holes in his chest that exposed his ribs and lungs. His blood-soaked hands clutched the AK that he had never fired.

The strikers moved among the VC, collecting their weapons and equipment. One man kicked the body of a dead VC. He stomped on the face and then, drawing his knife, bent down to cut the ears from the head.

Gerber watched but didn't stop him. He knew the MACV regulations that prohibited the mutilation of enemy dead, but they had been written by a leg who never got into the field. Mutilation of the dead was part of psychological warfare. Some Vietnamese believed that a mutilated man couldn't enter heaven and would be destined to walk the Earth forever. It was another way of fighting the war.

Besides, the dead man was dead. He didn't care what happened to his body. He didn't care about anything anymore. He was out of the battle.

Fetterman suddenly appeared out of the vegetation off to the right. "No one escaped?"

"Got them all," Gerber said.

Fetterman looked down at the body of one of the dead men. A bullet had shaved away the top of the skull, revealing part of the brain. "Now what?"

"Police up the weapons, equipment and documents and then move to the nearest LZ. Get the fuck out of here."

Fetterman looked at the captain. "You feeling all right?"

"Great. I just don't like ambushes."

"They're necessary."

"This isn't the place to discuss it," said Gerber. He turned and looked at the bodies and the strikers crouching over them.

"Any wounded?" asked Fetterman.

"None of our men. I think one VC managed to fire back, but all the rounds went into the canopy. We caught them completely off guard. VC are all dead."

"The plan worked," said Fetterman.

"Too easily," said Gerber. "Get your people in here and then take the point. I think we can hit an LZ about a klick to the south."

"Yes, sir."

As Fetterman moved off to complete his orders, Gerber turned to the rear. He slipped back into the jungle and crouched near the smooth trunk of a teak tree.

Maybe I'm getting too old for this, he thought. Once, he would have been elated by a perfectly executed ambush. Now he was sickened by the results.

MAXWELL WAS SITTING alone in his office when he heard a quiet tapping at his door. Without looking up from the report he was reading, he said, "Come on in."

General Hansen entered, followed by a full colonel and a first lieutenant. The general looked around, almost in distaste, then moved to the visitor's chair, sitting without waiting for an invitation. The colonel looked irritated that there was no chair for him. The lieutenant took a post near the door, almost as if trying to keep anyone from escaping into the hallway.

"Mr. Maxwell," said Hansen, "I was intrigued by something you said earlier."

Maxwell closed his report folder and turned to look at Hansen. "I didn't think you'd listened."

"I heard everything," said the general. "Sometimes it's necessary to pretend you don't because those under you begin to take an unhealthy interest in certain things."

"Meaning?" asked Maxwell, confused.

"Trying to please the general," said Hansen, "they run amok, doing and initiating activities designed to please me but that might not make good military sense."

Maxwell turned to face the man. He laced his fingers behind his head. "So, not wanting the lower-ranking officers at the meeting to know you were interested in the VC and NVA activity in Cambodia, you pretended it didn't bother you in the least."

"Something like that."

"So, what can I do for you?" asked Maxwell.

Hansen leaned forward and put an elbow on Maxwell's desk. "I want to stop the influence of the NVA in Cambodia."

"I told you in the briefing the most effective way of eliminating the influence."

Hansen closed his eyes and nodded. He seemed to be acknowledging Maxwell's statement while still appearing indifferent—a childish attempt at deception.

"Teams of two men as shooter and spotter and then a five-man security squad with the authorization to operate cross-border in Cambodia," added Maxwell.

"In violation of a dozen international agreements and laws," said Hansen.

"Of course, General," said Maxwell. He glanced at the other two men, neither of whom seemed interested in the conversation. Maxwell nodded at them. "Why don't they take a short walk?"

"They're authorized to hear everything that's said inside this office."

Maxwell reached for the phone. "Then you won't mind if I bring in a couple of my people, too."

"Why?"

"So that when the investigation is made it won't be my word against the three of you."

For a moment Hansen stared at Maxwell, trying to make the CIA man back down. When that failed, he laughed once. It was a single bark that held no mirth. Turning toward the colonel and his aide, he said, "Why don't you two occupy yourselves outside for the next few minutes?"

The lieutenant opened the door and waited for the colonel. Neither of them spoke as they left the office. As soon as the door was closed behind them, Hansen said, "Now lay it all out for me."

"The assassination of key Cambodian officers would throw the North Vietnamese plan into a cocked hat. With the death of those men, there would be an internal power struggle so that no one would be in a position to negotiate or assist the North Vietnamese."

"How can you be sure? You shoot Westmoreland and Abrams takes over immediately. No problem. You shoot a division commander and his deputy is the man in charge."

"Certainly," said Maxwell. "In the American Army. But you shoot General Tai of the Ninth AVRN Division and who takes over?"

"His deputy."

"Not necessarily," said Maxwell. "We're now dealing with an army where the officers can buy their commissions and rank. Tai dies, and it doesn't follow that Duong moves up. Someone from the outside might be able to influence the Saigon government and receive the promotion. Politics."

"Duong will still take over until the new man moves in."

"Maybe," said Maxwell. "Maybe not. The point is, the Ninth would be worthless as a fighting force for a week, ten days, or a month as the political games were played out. In Cambodia it's even worse."

"They buy their commissions?" asked Hansen.

"Hell, General, they steal them. It's the man with the biggest balls who ends up in command. There are men out there in command of battalions, regiments and divisions who have no loyalty to the government in Phnom Penh. They're in power because they took it, and their men obey their orders because they'll be shot if they don't."

"So if we have the information on who's leading which battalion or division and we shoot the top man, there'll be an internal power struggle to determine who takes command?"

"Precisely. With luck it would become so bloody that the unit would cease to exist. The men would run off into the night, abandoning their camp and leaders."

"How does this affect the North Vietnamese?" asked Hansen.

"They're making agreements with each of these generals. Individual agreements that aren't binding on the government in Phnom Penh."

"So why don't we alert the Cambodians to the problem and let them deal with it?"

Maxwell shook his head. "Because the Cambodians wouldn't deal with it. They'd ignore it. The only remedy is for us to take positive action."

"Even if we have to violate the neutrality of Cambodia to do it?"

"Look, General, the North Vietnamese don't give a shit about the neutrality of Cambodia. They operate inside Cambodia all the time. Why shouldn't we?"

"If we act like the enemy, if we descend to their level and ignore international agreements, we're no better than them."

"You can't fight a war with that attitude," said Maxwell. "You do what you have to do to win, and if you're not prepared to do that, then you get the hell out."

"I'll keep that in mind," said Hansen.

"General, war isn't a pretty business. It's not knights in armor riding out to do battle with other knights in armor. It's men and women doing everything they can think of to win, and if they don't play fair, they don't care because it's only the end result that matters."

"It's not how you play the game, but whether you win or lose," Hansen said cynically.

"That's exactly it. You don't remember the losers, only the winners."

"I don't agree with your point," said Hansen, "but I do agree that we have to take the Cambodian sanctuaries away from the enemy. You set up the teams and I'll approve the missions. But I want a full report from you on exactly what's going to happen and how it's going to happen." Hansen began to rise from his chair.

"One thing, General. I won't tell you a damn thing if you're going to confer with our South Vietnamese allies."

Hansen dropped back into the chair. "I don't appreciate minor functionaries dictating policy to me."

"And I'm not going to compromise the mission so that some South Vietnamese general can feel a part of the war effort. Every single ARVN unit has VC in it. Anything the ARVN know, the VC and NVA know."

"I want a full briefing."

"Fine, just don't tell the South Vietnamese what we're going to do until after we've done it."

Hansen closed his eyes again and nodded. Opening them, he said, "I can live with that. Now, how soon before your men can hit the field?"

"A week at the most."

Taking a deep breath, Hansen said, "Do it." He stood up, then moved to the door. As he opened it, he turned around. "I'm not fond of fighting a war this way."

"The men in the field aren't fond of doing it in any fashion," said Maxwell.

"Just keep me advised."

As the door closed, Maxwell picked up the phone, dialed a number, then attached the scrambler to it. When a voice on the other end answered, he said, "It's a go."

"Who are you going to contact first?"

"As soon as I'm done here, I'm going over to the SOG building and wait for Gerber and Fetterman. They'd be my first choice as a team."

"I have no problem with that. Who's their target?"

"A Cambodian general named Samphan. He's met with the NVA a couple of times and has pledged to support them. I'll have Gerber and Fetterman take him out."

"His replacement handy?"

"Standing by with the support to back him up in any power struggle."

"One of ours?"

"Been in deep cover for over ten years. He's in a perfect position to take over."

"Keep me posted on the progress of this operation," said the voice on the phone.

"Of course." Maxwell hung up and as he disconnected the scrambler, he wondered if his counter-part at the embassy realized the importance of this.

The CIA man smiled. With luck the missions, all seven of them, would be completed inside of two weeks and the back of the NVA in Cambodia would be quietly broken.

4

THE JUNGLE
NORTHWEST OF SAIGON

They made good time from the site of the ambush to the clearing that could be used as an LZ. Fetterman stopped the men at the edge of the jungle. It looked as if farmers had taken a giant knife and chopped off the jungle to create the rice paddies that were now spread out in front of them.

Gerber joined the master sergeant, crouching at the tree line. Clutching his M-16 in his left hand, he wiped at the sweat on his face, then rubbed his hand on the thigh of his jungle fatigues, leaving a ragged stain there. During the march from the ambush site to the LZ, he hadn't thought about the heat, the humidity and the danger of the jungle. He'd concentrated on getting away from the enemy. Now, with safety a few minutes away, he was overwhelmed by the heat and humidity.

"Nothing," whispered Fetterman.

"Security out?"

"Guys swinging around in both directions to make sure we're clear."

"This may not be the smartest move we've made. If there was someone around to hear the ambush, they might second-guess us and bring people in here."

"There's another LZ four klicks beyond this one," said Fetterman.

"Same problem," said Gerber. He was quiet for a moment. "Let's just secure this one, then I'll get on the horn and whistle up some choppers."

Fetterman nodded and disappeared into the thick green vegetation. Gerber turned his attention back to the open rice paddies. The dikes, no more than eighteen inches high, enclosed brown water that stank like an open sewer. He'd been surprised to see Vietnamese fishing in the paddies, figuring it was similar to the kids back home who fished in ponds, not because there was anything to catch, but because they wanted to go fishing and it was the only place available. And then he'd been even more surprised when the Vietnamese began to catch fish—flat, ugly things three or four inches long, but fish nonetheless.

Across the open paddies, a hundred meters away, was a clump of coconuts and palms, fifty or sixty feet high, and hidden in the shade, a couple of mud-and-thatch hootches which looked recently repaired, though there didn't seem to be anyone around them.

Gerber crawled forward until he could see the length of the landing zone. It was big enough for ten ships, even if they had to shoot long because of the tall trees at either end. The only obstructions were the farmers' hootches, and they presented no problems.

Fetterman reappeared then and crouched near Gerber. "Some abandoned bunkers on the north. No indications of any recent activity."

Gerber nodded, got to his feet and moved to the rear. The RTO was kneeling near a palm tree, leaning back against it, letting the trunk support his weight. Gerber walked to him, leaned close to check the frequency, then dialed in a new one. Taking the handset, he heard the tuning squeal as the radio cycled itself. Once it finished, he said, "Crusader Six, Crusader Six, this is Zulu Six."

There was a pause and then, "This is Six. Go."

"We're ready for pickup."

"Roger. Wait one." Then, "Say location."

Gerber crouched and jerked his map from his pocket. Using a grid system that had been designed by him and Fetterman, and then delivered to Crusader operations before the mission, he gave Crusader Six the LZ.

"Roger," came the reply. "We'll be inbound your location in one five minutes. Say condition of Lima Zulu."

"LZ is cold."

"Roger, cold."

Gerber waited, but there was nothing else. He gave the handset back to the RTO, then moved to the edge of the jungle where Fetterman waited. "Be about fifteen minutes."

"Yes, sir."

Gerber glanced at the farmers' hootches and then at the empty fields. The rice plants that poked up through the water looked well cared for, but then Gerber didn't know that much about rice cultivation. He did know there were periods during their growth when they didn't need much attention.

"I'm bothered by those hootches," said Gerber, keeping his voice low.

"No movement in them in the past few minutes," said Fetterman.

Gerber wiped a hand across his lips. "Charlie's not around the LZ. That's the logical place for him to be. I'd feel better if there were some people, farmers, moving around them."

"I could take a couple of strikers over to check it out," suggested Fetterman.

"That tips our hand. We lay chilly here and let the slicks come in, we might get out with no fire. We start farting around, we could find ourselves pinned down out there."

"Slicks bringing guns?"

"I would imagine," said Gerber.

"So how are we going to handle this?"

"Split the men up into loads, but keep them under cover in the trees. Throw smoke when we're asked to, advise Crusader Six to watch the hootches, then sprint on out."

"We could call artillery in on the hootches," said Fetterman.

"The problem is that there might be innocent people in there. We can't just indiscriminately call in artillery."

"I know, sir," said Fetterman. "It's a hell of a way to fight a war."

The RTO crawled up then, the handset held out in front of him. Gerber took it, listened for an instant, then said, "This is Zulu Six."

"Roger Six, we're zero five from your location. Can you throw smoke?"

"Roger, smoke." Gerber looked at Fetterman, who stood there with a smoke grenade in his right hand. Glancing at his watch, he said, "Give them about two, three minutes. Then let's get the men out of the trees and lined up in a staggered trail for the pickup."

Fetterman nodded and moved off to alert the striker NCOs. Gerber stood still, his eyes on the hootches near the center of the LZ. They still bothered him, though there was no indication that anyone was hiding in them.

Snapping his fingers, he took the handset back and said, "Crusader Six, this is Zulu Six. Be advised there is a cluster of hootches in the LZ and we've had negative opportunity to recon them."

"Are there people around them, Six?"

"We have negative knowledge of that."

"Roger."

The men began to filter out of the trees. They stepped over the short dikes and walked through the rice paddies. Most of them stepped on the young plants, using them so that they didn't sink into the muck at the bottom of the paddy. They splashed out into the open and then spread out, five men to a load separated by twenty or thirty meters so that the aircraft could land near them.

Gerber hesitated at the edge of the trees, watching the hootches across from him, but there was still no movement around them. The enemy, if they were there, would realize that Gerber's force was preparing for pickup. The real prize would be the landing choppers as they hovered ten or twelve feet above the ground. They'd become sitting ducks, waiting for the VC to shoot them full of holes.

Fetterman pulled the pin of his smoke grenade and tossed it onto a dike five feet away. There was a dull pop, a flame shot from the bottom and then a yellow cloud billowed upward.

The radio crackled to life. "ID yellow."

Gerber squeezed the handset. "Roger, yellow." He turned then and saw the choppers in the distance, little more than specks in the sky, the roar of the turbines an annoying buzz that slowly built.

Gerber gave the handset back to the RTO and then knelt down, one knee in the foul-smelling water of the rice paddy. He rested the butt of his weapon against his thigh and watched the hootches. But there was still nothing to see.

The choppers reached the edge of the jungle and were coming closer, slowing for touchdown. The gunships stood off to one side, the nose of the lead aircraft pointed at the cluster of mud-and-thatch hootches.

The men were now standing, their heads bent against the onslaught of the rotor wash, which rippled the water, pushing it toward the dikes. The pop of rotors and the roar of turbines filled the air.

As the lead chopper touched down, the skids settling into the water and disappearing, Gerber scrambled up into the cargo compartment. He slipped across it, leaving a slimy trail of mud behind him. Crouching in the cargo compartment door, he could see the hootches again. Still no movement from them. The door gunner sat quietly behind his M-60, the barrel pointed at the hootches just in case.

And then came the first stutter of a machine gun. Gerber couldn't spot it but did hear it over the roar of the helicopters. The door gunner reacted immediately, spinning toward the noise, but didn't fire.

AKs opened up then. The water around the choppers began to fountain and splash. There was a chugging from the trail aircraft. First an M-60 shooting back, and then M-16s as the strikers shot at the hootches.

The rest of the men in Gerber's load clambered aboard. As the last man stepped on the skid, the pilot pulled pitch. The aircraft leaped from the rice paddy, water cascading from the skid. They held at three or four feet for an instant, and then the nose dropped. Suddenly they were racing across the open fields, no more than a couple of feet high, the speed increasing rapidly as they fled.

Gerber grabbed the support for the troop seat and then leaned forward, looking to the rear. Now there was movement among the hootches. Men dressed in black carrying AKs were boiling out of one of the hootches. They scattered, knelt and opened fire, aiming at the remaining helicopters.

"I knew it," he shouted. "I fucking knew it."

The first of the gunship runs started then. The ground near the hootches erupted as the rockets hit. Twin explosions that seemed to walk from one end of the tree cluster to the other. Mushrooming explosions of black dirt and white smoke. Tracers erupting upward. Others coming down in a steady stream. One man was hit, knocked over and rolled away.

Gerber's chopper came up suddenly, gravity forcing him down like an express elevator that started up. He moved to the right and sat down on the troop seat, his hand still clinging to the support.

Behind him the thatch of the hootches was burning ferociously as white smoke poured from it. Enemy soldiers, now clustered outside, were firing up at the armed helicopters. An explosion among them tossed several of them to the side. One man broke and ran across a rice paddy dike. The water on either side of him boiled as M-60 machine gun rounds churned the paddies. Finally the man stumbled, ran a couple of steps, then sprawled into the dirty water, losing his rifle. He lay still, facedown.

And then the chopper was up and over the trees, the cluster of hootches now invisible. Only a column of white smoke marked their location.

Gerber moved forward, knelt by the map case at the end of the console between the pilots and yelled, "We going back into the LZ?"

The aircraft commander, a young, pimple-faced kid, turned, pulled the boom mike away from his lips and shouted back, "You want to return?"

"Got contact," said Gerber.

"Guns'll take care of it. Charlie can't get away from the hootches without the guns seeing him."

"Ground sweep to count the bodies and pick up the weapons," suggested Gerber.

"Got grunts on standby to do that, unless you feel a real need to go back in."

Gerber shook his head. "No reason," he shouted. With the guns working over the area, there would be nothing to see except the broken bodies of the enemy and shrapnel-riddled weapons to collect. A leg unit could do it as easily as any one. "You taking us to Saigon?" he asked.

"Hotel Three, if that's what you want."

"How about the SOG pad?"

"Where's that?"

"On Tan Son Nhut proper, not far from the Air America pad on the north side of the runways."

"No problem," yelled the pilot.

Gerber slipped to the rear and sat down on the troop seat. He took a position in the center, as far away from the doors as he could get. Leaning back against the gray soundproofing that covered the transmission wall, he listened to the rhythmic pop of the rotor blades and the hypnotic roar of the turbine. Now, in the helicopter, he was protected from the war. Safe for a moment, at fifteen hundred feet where the air was cooler and drier. They were outside the effective range of small arms, and Charlie rarely fired his .50s at helicopters during the day. It was too easy to be spotted and eliminated in the daylight.

He opened one eye and watched the strikers sitting on the deck, hanging on, some of them looking out as the land slipped away beneath them. Gerber didn't have to look because he'd seen it all before, more times than he cared to remember. Blurs of deep green that marked the jungle canopy. An unbroken sea of green that stretched to the horizon. Finally it would begin to thin, and then disappear as they approached Highway One. On the north side would be the Hobo Woods and rice paddies, and south of it would be a swamp, sometimes called the Plain of Reeds.

It was something he didn't have to see again. There was no reason to sit there, watching as the hamlets and villages appeared. No reason to look down on farmers who refused to look up, afraid it would draw the wrath of the warriors in the sky. There was nothing out there he wanted to see, nothing he hadn't seen before.

MORROW HAD ALREADY DECIDED she didn't like Danforth. He seemed to have made up his mind about everything, knew that the Army, the government and the South Vietnamese were lying about everything under the sun. Objectivity was dead. Long live Danforth.

But Hodges had retreated to his office, leaving her to talk to the new guy. Suddenly she understood why everyone who had just arrived in Vietnam was labeled an FNG. The fucking new guys thought they had the answers, though they hadn't understood the questions and hadn't bother to read the texts. They arrived, figuring they knew it all and were prepared to demonstrate it. In a combat situation, Morrow knew, that could get them killed, along with the old-timers. Here, it would just mean that biased, tainted reports would be put on the wire, satellite or plane to color the thinking of anyone who read newspapers or watched TV.

"So what are we going to do first?" asked Danforth, breaking into her train of thought.

Morrow glanced toward the office where Hodges hid behind his newspaper. She knew what he was doing. If she was going to rotate home, he was going to give her the shit assignments because she wouldn't be around to get even.

Standing up, she said, "Over to MACV so that you can see where the war is planned."

"Good," said Danforth. "I can't wait to get my teeth into this."

"Let's go easy on that investigative journalism stuff, shall we?"

"Why? You afraid I'm going to learn something that'll blow the lid off the war effort?"

"No. I'm afraid you'll alienate the sources and we won't be privy to anything. You have to cultivate your sources. Treat them like people, or they dummy up on you and you're stuck with your ass hanging out while everyone else is getting the really good stories."

"Shit," said Danforth.

Morrow stared at him. "Don't go burning my sources for me, then. I'll introduce you around, but don't get on that soapbox to preach about the morality of the war or the corruption that keeps it going. You smile and say, 'Glad to meet you,' and let it go at that."

"Sure," said Danforth.

Morrow bent and picked up her camera bag. "I mean this. You burn any of my sources and I'll have your balls."

"Nice talk," said Danforth, grinning broadly.

Morrow felt the rage boil through her. She wanted to reach out and smash his smug face. There was something about his voice, his attitude, about him, that rubbed her the wrong way. As he'd walked up to her desk, she had suspected it, and now she knew it. After sitting there, listening to him drone on and on, she'd known that she hated him. He made it so easy for her to hate him. It was a God-given gift.

"MACV first," said Morrow, trying to be civil. "And then downtown to find you a place to stay."

"I thought I could stay in your room," he said.

"Not if it was the only place available in the whole city," said said. "Not if you were wearing rags and on the verge of collapse."

"No, I mean if you're going home, it would be easier for me to take over there. I wouldn't have to search for something else. It'd do fine."

Morrow took a deep breath and mentally counted to ten, then twenty and finally thirty. She knew it was doing no good. She could count to a thousand and she'd still want to smash him. Gritting her teeth, she said, "Let's get going."

They left the city room and walked down the hall that had seen better days. The walls were stained, the paint faded. The carpeting had worn through to the floor in some spots, and there were only a couple of working lights creating pools of brightness. Danforth opened the thick metal front door, letting in a blast of sunlight and hot air.

"Is it always this hot?" he asked.

Morrow felt the sweat blossom the moment she stepped out onto the crowded sidewalk. She wiped a hand across her cheeks and forehead. "No. Sometimes it get real hot."

"So, how do we get to MACV?"

Morrow stepped to the curb and waved a hand without saying a word. A twenty-year-old multicolored Ford lurched out of the traffic and stopped near her with a squeal of brakes. She grabbed the hot handle of the rear door and said, "Take a taxi."

As Danforth climbed into the rear with her, Morrow said a final time, "Today you listen. Keep your mouth shut and listen and learn. Once you're out on your own, you can do anything you please."

"Yes, sir."

"Being a smartass isn't going to get you anything." She closed her eyes as the taxi pulled out into traffic. "MACV," she told the driver, and then wished Gerber was around. She really needed to talk to someone. Talk to him.

5

SAIGON

Even without opening his eyes, Gerber knew they were nearing Saigon. They had descended and were now approaching from the west. There was a new odor in the air—diesel fuel and gas fumes, and the stench of two, three million people living in a city that would have been crowded by a mere five hundred thousand.

Finally he opened his eyes and looked out over the tops of the buildings that made up Saigon. They were low buildings, two and three stories high, all with dung-colored walls and red tile roofs. Smoke hugged the grounds, some of it from cook fires built by the refugees, some caused by the burning of waste and some from the explosions of the random rockets and mortars lobbed into the city to frighten the people.

They came up climbing and then leveled off, skirting the edge of Hotel Three. They flew over the top of the World's Largest PX and then paralleled the taxiways, only a few feet off the ground, until they came to the SOG pad. There the pilot flared, hauling back on the nose, leveled the skid and then set down.

Gerber hopped out and ran to the side, keeping his head down. He turned his back to the chopper and felt the wind of the rotor against him. A moment later the flight lifted, followed the taxiway and disappeared. When they were gone the noise level fell off.

Gerber turned and saw Tyson leading the strikers across the road toward an open field. Braver stood there for a moment and then ran off, following Tyson and the strikers. Fetterman said something to Sergeant Thai, who nodded. Then the Master Sergeant headed toward Gerber.

"Tyson and Thai will get the weapons check made and then see about getting transport in to move them over to their permanent quarters," said Fetterman.

"Okay," said Gerber. "Good. Let's you and me check in and then see about getting into the city."

Fetterman pulled the magazine from his M-16 and then ejected the live round from the rifle. He stooped, picked up the bullet and shoved it back into the top of the magazine, which he dropped into his pocket.

Together they walked toward the front of the SOG building, a low single-story structure with a rusting, corrugated tin roof and wood and screen walls. Stacks of sandbags, three or four feet high, surrounded it.

Fetterman grabbed the wooden door handle, which was covered with clear plastic that had turned yellow during the months it had been up. Gerber stepped inside. The interior was air-conditioned, though the unit was old and inefficient. But the air was cooler inside, and it didn't seem quite as humid. The sweat that had covered them from the moment they'd stepped off the choppers on the tarmac began to evaporate.

Gerber hooked a thumb over his shoulder. "You want a Coke?"

"Coke would be great."

Gerber entered the dayroom. The small room held a single table with four chairs, a beat-up couch upholstered in a blue fabric that had been stolen from the Air Force, a rack of magazines and paperback books, a hot plate and a refrigerator with a noisy compressor. Gerber looked at the man sitting on the couch and then opened the refrigerator, taking out two cold cans. Glancing at the man again, he said, "Hi, Jerry. You waiting for anything in particular?"

Maxwell reached up and fingered his tie, which was hanging loose. "You and Fetterman."

"Fetterman and I just returned from the field. Minutes ago. We haven't had time to shit, shower or shave."

Maxwell stood up. "I need to talk to you about an upcoming mission."

Fetterman appeared in the doorway and Gerber tossed him a can. "We could meet you in your office, oh, some time next week," the master sergeant told Maxwell.

"Or month," said Gerber. "We're in no hurry." He set his weapon in the corner, opened his Coke and drank deeply. "In fact," he said, "I could live without a meeting at all."

"Look," said Maxwell, "I've been sitting here for a couple of hours. I need the two of you for a mission."

"But we don't need the mission," said Fetterman. He leaned against the doorjamb, refusing to enter. He sipped his Coke slowly and watched Maxwell.

The CIA man pulled his handkerchief from his pocket and mopped his face with it. He looked at the mud-and-sweat-stained fatigues that both Special Forces men wore, then stared at the nightmarish camouflage paint on their faces. "I know it's bad timing, but we've got something going. We need to make some plans and we need some fast action."

Gerber leaned against the front of the refrigerator. "Jerry, we're not the only two men in the Special Forces."

"No, but you're the best."

"Then give us a pay raise," said Fetterman.

Maxwell shook his head. He looked from one man to the other, then pulled out a chair and sat down so that he could watch both of them. "Can we stop fucking around. I'm tired, hot and not in the mood for this."

"Well, shit, Jerry," Gerber said, "pardon me all to hell. I didn't know we were inconveniencing you. We've just spent four days in the field, but hell, Jerry, we certainly don't want to inconvenience you."

"I'm getting tired of this," said Maxwell.

"Simple solution. Find someone else to do your dirty work, Jerry," said Fetterman.

Maxwell took a deep breath. "We all have our jobs to do."

Gerber drained his Coke, then set the can on top of the refrigerator. "If you don't have anything important to say to us, I'd like to clean my weapon and then check on the strikers. And I have to do all that before I even have a chance to take a shower."

"I wouldn't want to put you out," said Maxwell.

"Fuck it," snapped Gerber. "I'm tired of this game. Just tell us what you want, Maxwell."

Maxwell slammed the table with his hands, his face a mask of rage. He started to shout and then stopped. "I know it's not easy on you. I know there are Saigon commandos who spend every day in air-conditioned offices and every night in the bars chasing women. But my job isn't all that easy, either."

"Look, Jerry," said Gerber, "you have to understand that the last thing we want to see after we come in from the field is someone waiting around for a chance to send us right back out. We've got paperwork to file and there are follow-ups we need to make."

"Such as?"

"We took fire coming off the LZ," said Gerber. "Now we could have circled around and gone right back in, but the pilots thought their guns could handle the mission and they talked about some legs who would mop up, but I'd like to make sure that happened."

"I can take care of that for you," said Maxwell.

Gerber took a deep breath and then fished a second Coke out of the refrigerator, opened it, and then moved to the table. "Why don't you tell me what you need so that I can go take a shower?"

"You want to join us, Tony?" asked Maxwell.

"Not really." He stepped into the room and sat down. "Can we make this fast?"

"I can give you the preliminaries so that you can think about it and then meet with me in the morning." The CIA operative grinned. "See, it's not so bad."

"That remains to be seen," said Gerber. "You still haven't told us what it's about."

Maxwell leaned forward, lowered his voice and began to outline the problem. As he did, he didn't make either Gerber or Fetterman happy.

SAMPHAN FOLLOWED his men from their tiny camp through the jungle that was in places so thick it took them an hour to move a hundred feet. They reached an area where the jungle thinned and they could look out and down into South Vietnam, spread out no more than half a kilometer in front of them. They could tell it was South Vietnam because of the aircraft overhead.

Samphan didn't want to cross the border himself. He was afraid of the might of the Americans. Afraid of the artillery, the helicopters and the fighters. There were too many ways to get killed in South Vietnam.

Using binoculars that had been given to him by the North Vietnamese, Samphan surveyed the enemy territory. Just across the border was a drainage or irrigation ditch. It began at the border and wormed its way east until it disappeared into a finger of jungle. Samphan couldn't understand why anyone would want to build such a fancy ditch. It held water and seemed to serve no other purpose. There were no huts or enemy camps near it, so it was the perfect target for his men. They could sneak down, throw a dozen grenades into it and then run back. They could then claim they had attacked a structure in South Vietnam and that their attack had damaged it.

Samphan, trying to look like the generals he'd seen in pictures and in the movies, drew his pistol and held it in his hand. The binoculars were hung around his neck. He waved a hand and started down the gentle slope, working his way closer to South Vietnam.

As they approached what he believed to be the border, they heard voices. Quiet voices speaking Vietnamese. Samphan had pretended not to understand the language when the North Vietnamese had visited him, but that had been a trick. He could understand it, and speak it when he wanted to. Not well enough to fool a Vietnamese, but well enough to be understood by them.

Now, still playing soldier, he halted the men. He got down on his belly and found that the binoculars were in the way. Taking them off, he handed them to the nearest man. Then, without a word, he began crawling forward slowly.

He stopped abruptly. Through gaps in the trees and bushes, he could see a group of men sitting around talking. Some of them were armed, holding a variety of weapons—M-1s, carbines and a couple of M-16s. Samphan knew they were South Vietnamese soldiers, but they didn't look as if they were very well trained. No security, no guards and no interest in what was happening around them.

Samphan slipped to the rear and found one of his sergeants. He leaned close. "Puppet soldiers."

The man nodded. "Are we going to kill them?"

"Yes."

The man nodded and crawled off, searching for the other NCOs. As he moved, he could hear the quiet babble of the Vietnamese voices. It was obvious the enemy didn't know they were about to die.

The NCOs gathered around Samphan and looked expectantly at the general. He sat on the soft, wet ground, his pistol clutched in his hand. Now that he had their attention, he didn't know what to say. He wanted them to attack the South Vietnamese, but wasn't sure how to order them to do it. And he couldn't admit that because it would tell his soldiers that he wasn't capable as an officer. They'd leave him sitting alone in the jungle.

Instead he leaned close, pointed at one of the NCOs and said, "I shall let you have the honor of leading this mission. You will gain great glory in the destruction of the puppet soldiers from Saigon."

The NCO nodded and grinned with excitement. He was a young man, no more than twenty, who had gone east to fight the enemies of Cambodia. Now he was about to have an opportunity to kill South Vietnamese.

He gathered his men together and quietly instructed them. Four men to sneak around to the east as a blocking force. The rest of them to slip forward until they could see the enemy. He would throw a grenade, and as it exploded, they would all open fire, shooting everyone and everything that moved.

When he finished, he glanced at Samphan, who nodded his approval. He held his pistol and pointed toward the enemy. "Kill them."

The men split up. Samphan fell in with the NCO, crawling along behind him. As they approached the South Vietnamese campsite, they slowed, then began to work their way forward carefully on their bellies. Samphan felt a sudden thrill of fright. The skin on the back of his neck crawled and chills raced down his spine. It was like sneaking off into the jungle to meet a girl when he was a teenager. An exciting feeling because he didn't believe he would be killed in the next few minutes. It was a great thrill for him, going into combat, especially without a great deal of danger to him.

They stopped and listened to the South Vietnamese. They chattered as if they didn't have a care in the world. They laughed loudly. They smoked cigarettes. It was almost as if they thought they were out in the jungle for a picnic, not on a patrol.

The NCO rolled to his left and took out a Chicom grenade. He yanked the pin free and held the grenade up so that Samphan could see it. The general nodded. As he did, the NCO climbed to his knees and cocked his arm. He threw the grenade, then whipped around his AK, aiming into the enemy camp. He pulled the trigger as the grenade exploded.

There were screams of surprise from the South Vietnamese. One man stood up and was ripped by shrapnel from the grenade. His face disintegrated as he toppled onto his back.

Then everyone was shooting—AKs on full-auto. The noise was one long detonation. The bullets ripped through the jungle. Bits of leaf and bark rained down from the trees.

The South Vietnamese were caught in the fusillade. They didn't know what to do and they died. Two of them turned to run and were cut down. The others fell to the jungle floor. The Cambodians were up, standing and firing into the bodies. They kept firing and reloading and starting again until the bodies were shredded and the odor of cordite and hot copper hung heavy in the humid jungle air.

Slowly, one by one, the Cambodians stopped firing until it was quiet all around them. Each man thought he could hear echoes of the firing, but that wasn't true. Samphan, the last man to stand, advanced a step and then stopped. He pointed his pistol at the body of a South Vietnamese and then noticed the head was missing.

He turned and looked at the scattered weapons. His men were coming out of the jungle and began picking up the equipment, staying away from anything soaked in blood. In minutes they had stripped the bodies. Without a word, Samphan spun, heading back into Cambodia. The ambush, the weapons and the equipment they had gotten, and the few papers they had found, would prove to the North Vietnamese that he was a man to be watched. His power was extending, growing.

MORROW SAT IN THE OFFICE and listened to Danforth talk at length about the mood on college campuses around the United States. He talked about student protests against the war, student rights activists, the SDS and the Black Panthers. He spoke about stopping the war because it was immoral and ending racial discrimination because it was demeaning.

"And you know that black soldiers are dying in disproportionate numbers here?"

The officer, a major named Newman, sat there in his sweat-stained jungle fatigues and nodded slowly. He was a pasty white man with thick black hair and a new scar on his face. It was a long white thing that started on his chin, climbed up his cheek and ended near his left eye. It was the result of Tet and the VC running loose in the streets of Saigon, shooting everything that moved.

He held up his hand when Danforth said that black soldiers were dying faster than whites. "Where in hell did you get that one?"

"Everyone knows it."

Newman shook his head. "I don't know it. I see a lot of lily-white units in the field getting their butts shot off. I see a lot of white kids going home in body bags."

Danforth waved a hand as if trying to clear a slate. "I didn't say that white soldiers weren't in combat. Only that statistically, black soldiers are carrying a heavier combat burden than they should."

"And I'm saying you're full of crap," said Newman.

"Of course you would," said Danforth.

"What's the source of this knowledge?" asked Newman again. "You saying there are some racists in the Army? I'd have to agree. There are white racists and black racists. You saying we're making up combat assignments based on race? I'd have to disagree. Unless you can show me some figures. Unless you have some documented proof."

"Everyone knows that blacks are assigned to line units more frequently than whites."

Newman glanced at Morrow, who was sitting there trying to pretend she didn't know Danforth. "I thought you reporters were supposed to be objective. I thought you went out to learn the facts, not go out and preach them."

"I'm sorry," she said.

"Don't apologize for me," said Danforth.

Newman shook his head sadly. "I want both of you out of my office, now."

"But we haven't finished," said Danforth.

Newman spun and faced the wall, ignoring both of them.

Morrow stood up, but Danforth didn't. She reached out and slapped his shoulder. When he looked at her, she nodded at the open door. Together they left.

In the hallway Morrow said, ''I thought I told you not to burn a source for me.''

Danforth laughed. ''But didn't you see him squirm? I mention that fact about blacks and he squirms.''

Morrow stared at him for a moment, then quietly said, ''Newman was wounded in a firefight. He got hit trying to drag a black soldier out of the line of fire. Then another black soldier rushes out and drags him out of the line of fire. The black enlisted man grabs the white officer before helping another black soldier. That suggest something to you?''

''What?''

''There are no black soldiers in combat. There are no white soldiers. There are only American soldiers. When the shooting starts, race disappears.''

''Christ, they've gotten to you, haven't they?''

For a moment Morrow said nothing. She stared at the young man and wondered how he had gotten to be twenty-four years old. With his attitude, she was surprised he hadn't been killed long ago. ''Come on, we're getting out of here,'' she said.

''Why?''

''Because I don't want to expose any more soldiers to you. They have enough trouble worrying about the VC without having to worry about American journalists, too.''

''I don't understand you,'' said Danforth.

''Makes us even.''

6

Gerber and Fetterman listened to Jerry Maxwell with as much attentiveness as they could muster. Afterward, the two SFers cleaned their weapons, stored them in the SOG arms locker, then used the recently installed shower to wash the camouflage paint and the grime of the jungle from their bodies.

Gerber noticed that the shower featured a water heater. It was a gas-powered type, designed to heat the water of fifty-five-gallon drums in which trays and field mess kits were washed. Gerber figured that some wise guy NCO had stolen the heater from a leg outfit. But the water wasn't hot, nor even warm. It was tepid, which was at least better than cold.

Once they finished, they drew fresh uniforms from supply so that both of them looked as if they had just arrived in-country. But the clever man, the one who had survived more than six months in-country, would notice that both Gerber and Fetterman wore well-used jungle boots. They were the clue to a soldier's status; no combat soldier would give up a pair of boots that were broken in for the stiff leather of brand-new ones.

"We going to write the reports now?" asked Fetterman.

"Hell, no," said Gerber. "That bullshit was for Maxwell's benefit. Make him think we have work to do and he'll cut us some slack. Let Tyson and Braver do that."

"Then we should swing by the barracks and make sure they have the strikers settled in?"

Gerber finished drying his hair with a towel, then tossed it onto a pile of laundry. "Don't you trust them? They know what they're doing."

Fetterman grinned. "Captain, they're babes in the woods. New guys, fresh from the World where all is sweetness and light."

"They're still Special Forces. They know the score."

"All right," agreed Fetterman reluctantly. "So what are you going to do?"

"Collect my weapon, find a cab and head downtown. Then I'm going to find Robin and see if she wants to eat dinner."

"A fine plan. Room for me to tag along?"

Gerber stared at the master sergeant. "What's this? You asking permission to go along?"

"I don't want to intrude," said Fetterman.

Gerber scratched his face. "There something going on I don't know about?"

"No, sir. Nothing like that. I just thought you and Robin might like to be alone."

"And we shall," said Gerber. "But we'll want to eat, and there's no reason for you not to join us. Hell, bring a date. Bring Kit if you want."

"Oh, no, sir," said Fetterman. "I don't want to do anything to sabotage U.S.-Vietnam relations by getting the two of them together. We'll leave Miss Emilie at home tonight."

"Whatever," said Gerber, shrugging. "You ready?"

Fetterman nodded. They left the latrine, retrieved their weapons from the arms locker and then moved down the narrow hall to the acetate-covered door. Fetterman opened it, letting the humid air of late afternoon roll in.

Gerber walked out and stopped. Fetterman joined him and they headed for the gate. They passed the two-story barracks, protected by green rubberized sandbags.

"I could get us a jeep," said Fetterman.

"No. Then we'd have to take care of it and some smartass in Saigon would steal it. Let's just find a cab."

They walked on, passing men dressed in stateside fatigues or khaki uniforms. On base camps and fire bases and in the field soldiers wore nothing but jungle fatigues, though the pilots sometimes wore flight suits. In Saigon, however, the men wore the same uniforms they would in the United States.

There were even Air Police who handed out discrepancy reports to soldiers whose uniforms were less than perfect. Soldiers coming in from the field were stopped by the APs and told they were a disgrace.

Gerber had seen one AP spend ten minutes writing out a report on a soldier who had obviously come in straight from the field. When the AP was finished, he handed the document to the soldier who read it quickly, tore it into tiny fragments and jammed it down the front of the startled AP's shirt. He'd then strolled away as if nothing had happened.

They reached the front gate, a sandbagged structure with an M-60 mounted in the middle of the sandbags. There were bunkers covering the approach, the Air Force's late response to the Tet attacks. At the gate were long lines of people, mostly Vietnamese, and mostly female, who were trying to get into the base. They were the women who would work in the clubs, serving soldiers and airmen, dancing, cleaning up or selling themselves for quickies in the back rooms.

Fetterman stopped and looked at the long line of women. Nearly all of them wore short skirts and see-through blouses. Their long black hair was pulled back off their round faces.

They looked like clones of one another. Faceless, feature-less women moving in on the nameless, faceless GIs. In a year the faces would all change, but the game would be the same.

"I find this lineup depressing," said Gerber.

Fetterman looked up at the captain, wondering if he had read his thoughts. "Depressing?"

"Let's get a cab and get out of here."

They spotted a cab letting four GIs out. Fetterman waved a hand and hurried forward, grabbing the door before the driver could disappear into the traffic. Gerber joined him and they climbed into the back seat.

"Where you go?" asked the driver.

"Carasel," said Gerber.

The driver popped the clutch, hit the gas and screeched into the traffic. There was a squeal of brakes, a blast from a horn and a few shouted obscenities, but then they were in the flow of traffic.

"Well, that woke me up," said Gerber.

"Better than a roller coaster," said Fetterman. He leaned back in the seat.

They hit the downtown streets, which were choked with traffic and pedestrians. Men and women, American and Vietnamese, wandered around, looking for a way to spend the evening that would help them forget where they were and what they did during the day.

There were also military vehicles on the street—trucks and jeeps and a couple of staff cars. Many of the civilian vehicles should have been scrapped years earlier. There were cars painted a rainbow of colors with rusty primer showing through and motor scooters ridden by reckless young men. The cowboys on the scooters weaved and dodged through the traffic, barely avoiding collisions with trucks and cars, while young women clung to their waists, seemingly oblivious to danger.

Gerber watched the traffic for a moment, and then, as he'd done in the helicopter, closed his eyes. He'd seen everything before. Gangs of GIs prowling, looking for a good time, trying to get the clothes off Vietnamese whores right there on the street. Gangs of Vietnamese youths prowling, looking for ways to separate the GIs from their money.

There was a sudden blare of horns, and the cab swerved to the left, back to the right and then stopped, almost throwing Gerber and Fetterman into the front seat.

"We here," announced the driver.

"Barely," said Fetterman.

Gerber opened the door and climbed out. Fetterman remained in the cab, arguing about the fare with the driver. Finally Fetterman pulled some MPC from his pocket and handed them over.

As he got out of the cab, Gerber asked, "How much do I owe you for the ride?"

"Forget it, sir."

"Nope," said Gerber. "You always pay for the cab because you always argue with the drivers."

"Trying to keep the economy in balance and the rate of inflation down."

Gerber shook his head. He didn't want to hear Fetterman's lecture on how it was the responsibility of each soldier to help keep the inflationary spiral in check by refusing to pay inflated prices for anything. The lecture usually covered the range from cab rides to the night when First Cavalry Division had single-handedly raised the price of a good whore from a buck to five bucks by blowing into town with pockets bulging with money and their hormones racing. They hadn't stopped to negotiate. If the whore said two bucks, they paid. If she said five bucks, they paid, and almost overnight every working girl knew she could get five times what she had gotten the day before.

They entered the hotel, where the doorman held out his hand as he opened the door for them. Gerber dropped an MPC dollar into his hand. The interior of the hotel was all marble and teak. In its day, before World War II, it had been a first-class hotel in a city that had rivaled Paris for beauty. But years of war had taken their toll.

They walked across the marble floor past the Victorian furniture that was now beginning to show its age. The wing-backed chairs and couches standing on clawed feet were arranged as conversation centers. Toward the rear was a long desk of dark wood. Several Vietnamese clerks worked behind it. Gerber and Fetterman retrieved their keys from one of the clerks. No one carried a hotel room key into the field.

With keys in hand, they headed to the elevator at the rear of the massive lobby. The car looked like a gilded cage and climbed a pole so that passengers could look down on the lobby until they were above the fifth floor.

Fetterman worked the buttons and Gerber stood in the corner, not saying a thing. "Meet for dinner in a hour?" the master sergeant asked.

"In the lobby," said Gerber.

"Of course."

FETTERMAN WAS SEATED on a couch, reading the *Stars and Stripes* when Gerber approached him. Fetterman sensed him coming and lowered the paper, looking over the top. "Says here that General Westmoreland is scheduled to turn command over to General Abrams in the next couple of days."

"Not a good thing for us," said Gerber. "Abrams doesn't like the Special Forces."

"Not hard to understand," said Fetterman, folding his paper. "Abrams is from the old Army. Tank driver in the Second World War who now finds himself in command of half a million men fighting a war he doesn't understand. The SF seems to typify everything that's wrong in this war.''

"Well, as I said, it's not a good sign for us." A movement distracted him, and he saw Morrow approaching. She was dressed in a light-colored blouse and a short skirt. Trailing along behind her was a young man.

"I see you two are ready." She glanced over her shoulder and asked, "You don't mind if I bring someone else along tonight, do you?"

Gerber shook his head. "Not at all."

Morrow stepped back to let Danforth move forward. "Captain Mack Gerber, this is Jason Danforth, newest member of the Fourth Estate. Jason, this is Captain Gerber and Master Sergeant Anthony B. Fetterman."

Fetterman held out a hand, "Tony, to my friends."

Danforth shook his hand but didn't say anything. A silence descended over them.

Morrow shifted her weight from foot to foot nervously, watching as the three men sized up one another. Finally, afraid they would come to blows if no one said anything, she said, "Jason arrived in-country this morning."

Fetterman nodded. "Skirts as short as they were?"

"Shorter now. Way above the knee."

"I don't think we have to get into a fashion discussion here," said Morrow.

"It's a subject I find interesting," said Fetterman.

"I thought we'd eat here, if there are no objections," said Gerber.

Morrow moved toward him and took his arm. She leaned close and smiled at him, telling him quietly that it had been her job to shepherd the new guy around. That was the only reason he was here.

"Upstairs is fine," said Morrow.

They moved toward the elevator. As they did, Gerber asked, "Anything new going on?"

Morrow glanced up at him and then shook her head. "Nothing except breaking in the fucking new guy."

They bypassed the elevator, turned a corner and climbed a wide set of stairs that curved off to the left. There was a chandelier hanging over the foot of the stairs, lighting the red carpeting that once might have glowed crimson, but that was now dull and stained from decades of hard use.

They climbed the stairs and moved down a wide hallway that was also brightly lit. It was a short corridor that ended in two mahogany doors with frosted glass windows. Gerber pushed on one of the doors and said, "This is a little more expensive than the other restaurants, but the service is the best and it's the quietest. Sometimes it's worth the extra dough."

As they entered, the maître d' intercepted them. Fetterman slipped him a bill, an American greenback rather than MPC, and they were escorted to a table immediately. It was a good one, with a view of the city and away from the kitchen and the entrance. There was a red cloth on the table along with white napkins, silverware and crystal glasses. Flowers in a cut-glass vase stood in the center, adding to the riot of color.

There were gaslights on the walls, but the flames had been replaced by small, clear bulbs. A couple of small chandeliers added to the brightness of the room. Red flocked wallpaper covered the walls.

Fetterman ordered a bottle of wine, then sat back to study the menu left by the waiter. Gerber pushed his aside and looked at Morrow. "You seem tired."

"Long day. Lots of long days. And you don't look that wide awake yourself."

He grinned. "Lots of long days."

Fetterman tossed his menu aside and glanced over at Danforth. "You just arrive today?"

"This morning."

"Then you must be worn out. Jet lag and all."

"Nope," said Danforth. "Got plenty of sleep on the plane, and there's been so much to do here that I haven't had a chance to feel worn out."

"We made it over to MACV this afternoon," said Morrow.

"See any signs of the big change-of-command ceremony?" asked Gerber.

Morrow shook her head. "We just visited a few offices and then headed back to the hotel to get young Jason settled in."

Danforth picked up the cue. "You guys are in the Green Berets?"

"No, Jason," said Morrow. "You let it lie now."

Gerber grinned. "The green berets are our hats. We're in the Special Forces, if that's what you mean."

"That's what I mean. Baby killers."

Fetterman laughed. "You trying to pick a fight already?"

"No, just trying to learn what's going on here in Vietnam. Story I hear is that all you Green Berets are real killers."

"Where'd you hear that?" asked Gerber.

"Everywhere. See it on the TV and read it in the newspapers. You're a ruthless lot who enjoy killing."

Gerber shot a glance at Morrow. "This clown for real?"

She shrugged. "I tried to tell him, but he wouldn't listen. Been here twelve hours and already he's alienated half the MACV staff. Now he's working on Special Forces."

"I'm just telling you what I've heard," said Danforth. "If I'm wrong, it's up to you to convince me."

"Whatever happened to the objective reporter?" asked Fetterman.

"That's what I wanted to know," said Morrow, "but he wouldn't tell me."

"I've seen the pictures," said Danforth. "Green Berets with their Zippo lighters, setting fire to the thatch roofs of Vietnamese homes."

"No!" said Gerber, slamming a hand on the table. "You haven't seen pictures of Special Forces troopers doing that. Legs, grunts, nineteen-year-old kids who were drafted to fight a war they probably hadn't heard about, given sixteen weeks of half-assed basic training and a rifle. You've seen them, after watching friends die because of booby traps and snipers, trying to get even. They've set those fires. But not Special Forces."

"Oh," said Danforth. "I suppose you're different."

Now Fetterman took over. "You're damn right we're different. Years of training—"

"In killing," interjected Danforth.

"Yes," agreed Fetterman. "Some of it in killing, but the majority of it in fighting a guerrilla war. Something the Army doesn't completely understand, but that we do. We teach the people how to defend themselves, but we also teach them the value of digging a latrine downstream and not up. Something you probably haven't figured out yet.

"And we build schools. We hold weekly sick calls, introducing them to antibiotics and preventive medicine. We teach them better methods of growing crops so that there's more food. We try to bring them out of the Stone Age and into the modern world without destroying them in the process."

"Sure," said Danforth. "Why don't I see that on the news or read about it in the paper?"

"Good question," snapped Gerber. "Why doesn't anyone report that?"

"Maybe because," said Fetterman, "bad news is more sensational than good. Who cares that Special Forces medics treated a hundred, two hundred, a thousand people today? But let one Special Forces trooper shoot a woman who was probably carrying a rifle and it's front-page news."

"All I know," said Danforth, "is that Special Forces troops have been guilty of some of the most heinous atrocities in this illegal war."

"Robin, where did you find this asshole?" Gerber growled.

She shrugged helplessly. "I warned him."

"And you," said Gerber, "I want you to give me the specifics of one atrocity commited by the Special Forces."

"I don't know of any offhand," replied Danforth.

"Right," snorted Gerber. "You can sit there and condemn men you don't know. You can spout off about atrocities, but have no facts to back you up."

"I saw the footage of the soldiers using their Zippos to burn that village."

"Regular Army soldiers. Not Special Forces."

"The same thing."

"Bullshit. It's not the same thing. Take some time to learn the facts. Have American soldiers committed atrocities? No doubt. But stack that up against what the Vietcong and the North Vietnamese have done. Where's your moral outrage at that?"

"That's between the Vietnamese."

"Oh, the murder of women and children isn't murder when it's committed by the Vietcong and North Vietnamese?"

"That's not what I said."

"That's exactly what you said." Gerber shook his head. "I don't understand it. I hear people saying it all the time. I read it in the paper and in the magazines, but I don't understand it."

"I'm just trying to learn what's going on here," said Danforth.

"No," said Fetterman. "You're looking for proof that you're right. You're not interested in learning anything."

Gerber slid back his chair. "Robin, I'm not going to eat with this jerk. If you have to stay, I understand, but I don't have to."

Fetterman stood up and headed toward the door without a word. Gerber hesitated a moment longer, then spun on his heel, following the master sergeant.

Morrow plucked the napkin from her lap and threw it on the table. "You handled that brilliantly."

"A little touchy for soldiers, aren't they?"

"Mr. Social Grace. Have a nice dinner." She took off after Gerber.

7

THE CARASEL HOTEL

The knock on the door didn't surprise Gerber. He figured that Morrow would stay with her FNG just long enough to cut him to ribbons and then she would be on her way up to his room. He'd had just enough time to open his wardrobe, drag out a bottle of Beam's and pour himself a couple of fingers into a glass.

The knock came again just as he was opening the door. Morrow pushed past him into the room and headed straight for the open wardrobe. She picked up the bottle, drank from it, then asked, "You have a glass?"

Gerber held up his. He dropped into the single chair and propped his feet on the bed. The air conditioner, built into the wall under the window, was just beginning to pour cold air into the room. He'd turned it on when he'd entered a few minutes earlier.

The room itself wasn't much—a double bed, a wardrobe instead of a closet, a chair and table, which held the small black-and-white TV he'd bought a few weeks earlier, and a bathroom off to one side. All the conveniences of a motel in the World with the added attraction of mortar shells and rockets.

Morrow walked into the bathroom and came out with another glass. She poured some Beam's into it, then sat on the edge of the bed, crossing her legs slowly. "So, what are we going to do about dinner?"

"That's a good question. But I've got a better one. Why were you saddled with that jerk?"

Morrow took a big drink of the bourbon. "I was going to break this to you gently. Slowly. Danforth is my replacement."

Gerber finished his drink.

"You're not surprised?" she asked.

"You've hinted about it for the past few weeks. I didn't know it had gotten that far. I mean, that you had a replacement coming in."

"He's not really my replacement," she confessed, "though if I decided to pull out tomorrow, the staff wouldn't be left shorthanded."

Gerber said nothing.

"You're not reacting."

"I don't know what to say."

"Men always have that problem. Say what's in your heart. Say what you feel."

Gerber smiled. "Easier said than done." He glanced at her. Long blond hair, brushed carefully and falling to her shoulders. A light silk blouse and a short skirt that stopped well up her thighs. She wasn't wearing stockings now, either. Just her bare skin showing.

"Tell me what you really want," she said, her voice suddenly husky.

Gerber turned and set his glass down on the table next to the TV set. "It's hard to talk of feelings," he said. "Very hard."

"Macho men don't jeopardize their status as macho by expressing themselves."

"No, it's not that. I'm torn between two emotions. One says let her go. Get her the hell out of Vietnam before she gets herself killed. The other says have her stay."

"Why stay?" she asked, uncrossing her legs and then re-crossing them slowly.

"You're going to make me say it, aren't you?"

"Hell, Mack, why not? Is it that much to ask? Just a few words to let me know what you feel."

"Do you really have to hear the words?"

"No," she admitted. "I don't have to, but I'd like to. Just once I'd like to hear them."

"You set on going home?"

She shrugged. "I don't know. Everything seems to be the same. The stories I'm doing today are the same ones I was doing last week. Stories of South Vietnamese soldiers failing and having to be bailed out by American soldiers. More Americans dying everyday and no one with a good answer as to why they have to die."

"Robin, you don't want to get into a debate about the role of the American soldier, do you?"

"No. I'm just telling you what I feel. I'm getting tired of it. Tired of all of it. And young Danforth seems to show us how well we've been doing our jobs. He blows in here with dozens of opinions picked up from television and newspapers. Tells me that I'm not doing my job."

"Or that I'm not doing mine."

"No," she said. "Your job isn't public relations. Your job is to fight the enemy, whoever that might be. But I keep filing stories about the good being done here and no one seems to be publishing them or reading them."

Gerber was suddenly uncomfortable with the discussion. He didn't like the direction it had taken, or that Morrow had asked him to tell her how he felt. He'd rather show her. He didn't like saying the words. He thought it made him vulnerable, though he couldn't have explained the feeling if asked. Changing the subject, he asked, "What about dinner?"

"I'm not hungry anymore. I never was hungry."

"I'd like to get something," said Gerber. "I've been in the field for the past few days eating C-rats. I wouldn't mind finding a thick steak and a baked potato."

Morrow glanced at him, then slowly reached down to her knee and drew her fingers up her thigh, hiking her skirt higher. She uncrossed her legs, and her knees were apart. "You really want to find a steak?"

"This an either/or question?"

"No. I just wanted to see your reaction."

"In that case, why don't we get something to eat, and then come back here? Then I'll show you a proper reaction."

Morrow stood and tugged at the hem of her skirt, though it didn't do much good. There wasn't that much material in it. "By the way, you don't fool me. I know you changed the subject without saying the words."

"Wouldn't it seem artificial now? Wouldn't you rather I said it on my own, when I'm ready to say it?"

"Okay, Mack, I'll let you go with that. But remember one thing, I say one word to Hodges at work and I can be on the next plane out of here, and then it'll be too late."

Gerber moved toward the door and grinned. "I can always write to you."

"You could, but then I don't have to open the letter." She pushed past him and out into the hallway. "Let's get this meal over quickly."

"Fine with me," said Gerber.

THE QUIET TAPPING on the door brought him out of a deep sleep quickly. Gerber's eyes snapped open and he rolled to the right, staring at the clothes littering the floor of the hotel room. He reached for his weapon, then realized where he was. Without a thought, Gerber threw back the sheet and snagged his underwear off the floor. Hopping on one leg, he hurriedly slid on his underwear, unlocked the door and retreated.

Fetterman pushed it open and stepped inside. "Morning, Captain. I wake you?"

Gerber yawned, his jaw cracking. "Of course you woke me. No big deal."

Stooping, Fetterman grabbed a pair of flimsy bikini panties from the floor. He held them up. "Yours?"

"Stop being stupid," said Gerber.

At that moment Morrow walked into the room, a towel around her wet hair. She stopped, looked at Gerber, then Fetterman, and froze. She didn't know whether to try to cover her naked breasts or crotch, so she did neither. Instead, she grinned broadly. "Excuse me."

As she whirled, almost leaping back into the bathroom, Fetterman said, "Excuse me."

"Well, that was pleasant," said Gerber.

"Didn't mean to walk in on anything, Captain," said Fetterman, "but we did promise to meet Jerry this morning."

Gerber nodded toward the bathroom door.

"I'm not worried about Miss Morrow overhearing anything," said Fetterman. "She's friendly."

"Neither am I," said Gerber. "But I am worried about that FNG she was dragging around. The wrong word in the wrong place, and he's going to be off on some tangent."

"Understood." Fetterman hesitated. "Why don't I meet you downstairs for breakfast in about fifteen minutes?"

"Why don't I meet you at the front door? We'll head over to MACV and see if we can't con Jerry into buying us breakfast."

"Of course," said Fetterman.

Gerber let the master sergeant out, then walked to the bathroom door. He tapped on it and asked, "You about done?"

She opened up but was now wearing a towel that covered her, almost. "Oh, Mack, I was so embarrassed." She stared at him, then began giggling.

Gerber couldn't help laughing. "It was nothing that Tony hasn't seen before. Besides, I thought you handled it perfectly."

"Perfectly," she said.

FETTERMAN WAS STANDING just inside the door, gazing out into the busy streets of Saigon as Gerber approached. "It never ceases to amaze me."

"What?" Gerber asked.

"The spectacle of the people here. They're all living on the brink. A bad day by the American military, and Saigon could be swarming with VC and NVA. Hundreds, thousands, could be dead in the blink of an eye, and they're all out there hustling as if nothing was wrong."

"What do you expect?"

Fetterman shrugged. "Something a little more substantial, I guess. They're all fiddling while they should be planning for the future. They can't see beyond the end of their noses and immediate gratification of their needs. As long as they have a full belly and a place to stay for the night, they're happy as clams."

"People have always been like that. Take care of now and the future will take care of itself."

"Granted. But here, with the enemy at the gates, so to speak, you'd think people would have thought their way through the problem. What happens if we suddenly pulled out tomorrow? No American military might to prop up the Saigon government and the South Vietnamese army?''

"The people would adapt immediately to the new situation," said Gerber. "Or they'd die. But then we're not pulling out tomorrow."

"No, sir," said Fetterman. "Not tomorrow."

Gerber pushed open the door and stepped into the street. The heat, humidity and odors of Saigon assaulted him. He lifted a hand to shade his eyes until they were used to the brightness of the sun reflecting off stone buildings and paved streets.

Fetterman joined him, and they spotted a taxi sitting at the curb. The master sergeant climbed into the back and said, "MACV."

The driver nodded, waited until Gerber entered, then used his turn signals to alert the traffic of his intentions. When there was a hole, he slipped into it, accelerating slowly and smoothly.

Gerber leaned close to the master sergeant. "What's happening here? This guy knows how to drive."

"Sit back and enjoy," said Fetterman.

They made their way through the city past a police stand at the intersection of the streets. A Vietnamese in a white helmet stood blowing a whistle that only a few people paid attention to. Music blared from the bars, open already, accommodating the GIs who had to get all their living crammed into two or three days before they returned to fire bases and patrols into the jungle. The bar girls were already out in force, trying to find companionship for the day so that they wouldn't have to work so hard.

They pulled into the parking lot, the tires crunching on the gravel as they slowed. The driver stopped next to the sidewalk, turned and grinned. "Made it, gents. About five hundred P."

Fetterman reached for his wallet, but Gerber stopped him. "Why five hundred P?"

"Hell, my man, I could ask for a thousand. You'd offer two. We dicker around and finally agree on something around five hundred. Depending on everyone's mood, I might get a little more or a little less, but this is a fair price."

"True," said Gerber. "And your command of English is extraordinary. Can you speak Vietnamese as fluently?"

"I grew up in San Francisco. My father was a diplomat, so I speak French, English and Vietnamese fluently."

"You wouldn't like a new job?" asked Gerber.

The driver laughed. "And give this up?" He shook his head. "Seriously, I'm my own boss, set my own hours and no one is trying to kill me. I'll pass."

"If you change your mind, my name's Gerber. Ask around here or leave a message and someone will get it to me."

He climbed out of the cab and it drove off. Fetterman watched it go, then looked at the captain. "You think it was smart giving him your name?"

"Hell, he could read it off my fatigues. He knows I'm a captain and that we're Special Forces. He knew that and neither one of us had to say a word."

"True."

They walked up the sidewalk and around the flagpoles that held American and South Vietnamese banners hanging limply in the humid air. Flowers in deep reds, yellows and blues grew at the base of the poles. Off to the right soldiers walked across an expanse of green lawn, picking up cigarette butts, tin cans and discarded paper.

"I wonder where all the trash comes from," said Gerber as they reached the double doors leading inside. "The enlisted men don't throw it around because they'll have to pick it up. The NCO's don't because they've spent years cleaning it up. And the officers don't because it'll set a bad example. And yet somehow it always gets thrown out there for someone to pick up.''

Fetterman opened the door. ''My theory is that the NCOs do it on purpose so that the enlisted men will have a reason to be out there. Makes work for the NCOs, first in creating the trash, then supervising the men as they clean it up. And it makes work for the men. Everyone's happy because everyone gets to bitch about it.''

''I should have known you'd have an answer,'' said Gerber. ''You always have an answer.'' He entered the building. Cold air attacked him, and he shivered once, then felt the sweat begin to dry quickly.

''Down to Maxwell's office first?'' asked Fetterman.

''Unless you want to go in search of doughnuts, since we didn't eat breakfast.''

''I can wait,'' said Fetterman.

They walked along the green tiled hallway to the stairs that led down into the basement. Near the bottom of the steps was an iron gate with an MP sitting behind it. He had a small desk and a roster. When Gerber and Fetterman approached, he looked up. ''Can I help you?''

''Captain Gerber to see Mr. Maxwell.''

''Yes, sir.'' The MP checked the access roster, found Gerber's name, then asked, ''You have ID?''

Gerber handed the man his green military ID card. The MP accepted it, looked at the picture, then at Gerber. ''Serial number.''

Gerber gave it.

''Fine, sir.'' He glanced at Fetterman. ''Sergeant?''

Fetterman went through the same routine with the man. Finished and satisfied, he opened the gates, then pushed the clipboard at them. ''Please sign in with the date and time.''

Gerber bent over, signed in, then handed the pen to Fetterman, who did the same. Finished, they hurried down the narrow hall with the dirty tile, stained by rust marks showing where files and metal bookcases had once stood.

Stopping at Maxwell's door, they knocked. A moment later the door opened and Maxwell said, "Come on in." He turned, leaving them standing in the hallway until they decided to follow him.

As always, Gerber sat in the visitor's chair. Fetterman moved to the filing cabinets and leaned against the top. Neither of them spoke.

Maxwell walked to his desk and tried to casually cover the secret document he was working on. Both Gerber and Fetterman knew what he was doing. They'd been around long enough to have seen others try to casually hide classified material and not be obvious about it.

Finally Gerber said, "We've thought over your proposition and decided the answer has to be no."

For a moment Maxwell sat there, staring down at the top of his desk. Then he began to laugh. "No? You actually think you have a choice in the matter?"

"Of course we do," said Gerber.

"What about your military training? Riding into the valley of the shadow of death and all that?"

Fetterman took over. "You have us confused with the Light Brigade."

"But orders," said Maxwell.

"Jerry, let's cut the crap," Gerber said. "You know as well as we do that we're obligated to obey lawful orders. If we were in a movie now, there'd be talk of direct orders and all that, but we aren't. We're here, where our only concern is lawful orders. Orders that don't violate the laws of the United States, international law or military law. Everything else is unlawful, and we don't have to obey them."

Maxwell nodded. "These are orders approved by your superiors."

"Doesn't make them lawful," said Fetterman.

"You'd both be court-martialed."

Now Gerber laughed. "You know, that might work against someone who was new to the Army. Might scare the teenagers fighting in the fields, but Sergeant Fetterman and I have been around a lot longer. We know that a court-martial works for us as well as it does for you."

"Meaning?"

"That no one's going to court-martial us for refusing to sneak into Cambodia to smoke some minor official. That would violate a number of laws."

Maxwell leaned back in his chair and laced his fingers behind his head. He stared at the cinder-block wall in front of him, at the moisture beading on it as the heat of the day built outside. "Lawful orders will be issued," he said finally.

"Just like the last time?" asked Fetterman. "Lawful orders were issued and I found myself in LBJ accused of murder."

"Different time and different circumstances," said Maxwell.

Gerber stood up and glanced at Fetterman. "I think we'll take a pass on this."

"You can't," said Maxwell.

"We damn well can," said Gerber. "You just watch us."

8

THE CARASEL HOTEL

When Gerber and Fetterman left, Morrow dressed, then slipped up to her own room. It was a carbon copy of the one occupied by Gerber, except that hers had a tiny kitchen. A small table that she used as a desk was shoved into one corner of the room. A portable typewriter sat on one end, and the rest of the table top was covered by a mountain of papers—stories she'd started and not finished, bits of a novel she claimed she was writing, notes for stories to come and scraps of stories she'd ripped apart because she didn't like them.

She'd changed into a jumpsuit, then dropped into the chair near the bed. She felt exhausted, used up, tired, and knew it had nothing to do with Gerber and what they'd done the night before. Glancing at the air conditioner, she wished she had turned it on before sitting down, but now didn't have the energy to do it.

Taking a deep breath, she asked, "What am I supposed to do now?" There was no answer, just the muted noise of the traffic on the streets below her, the quiet roar of a jet overhead and the rhythmic thump of the bed in the next room, accompanied by moans of pleasure.

The images, the sounds, the sights and the feelings were all things from her past. She knew what each day would bring. She knew it would be hot and humid and filled with death. The reporters would fight to get the best pictures of the death and destruction, and the Army would try to paint a happy face on everything. The governments, both Vietnamese and American, would be less than candid with the public.

Suddenly agitated, she stood and walked to the window. She slammed her hand against the air conditioner, hitting the On button. Cool air blew out at her. To her reflection in the window, she said, "Less than candid, hell. They're lying to everyone about everything all the time."

The knock at her door didn't surprise her. She leaned an ear against the door and waited. The knocking came again, but no one spoke. She whipped open the door and saw Danforth, who was dressed in khaki, as if he were an African big game hunter. He had his hand raised to knock again.

"Morning, Robin," he said.

"Hi." She whirled and walked into the center of the room.

Danforth followed her. He moved to the window and looked out at Saigon. "Strange city," he said.

"Look, Danforth, there are a couple of things we need to get straight."

He held up a hand to stop her. "I know I came on a little strong yesterday. I didn't mean to. It's just, well, I've been in college for four years and then worked for my father's paper. I had no chance to get out and do something of substance. I had to sit back and watch everyone else do important work, so I was wound a little tight yesterday."

"Captain Gerber and Sergeant Fetterman are two of the finest men I know."

"Even if they're Green Berets?"

"Don't go throwing around terms you don't understand. The media, meaning us, is fond of labels. Makes our job easier. We don't have to think of descriptions or words to make the reader understand. We use the label and most time those labels aren't accurate."

"You like them, don't you?"

"What's that got to do with it?"

Danforth shrugged. "If you like them, then your opinions and your reporting might be less than objective, especially concerning them."

"You don't have to hate your sources to be objective."

"No," agreed Danforth.

Morrow looked at her watch. "We'd better get going. We'll check in and then go over to the embassy. And this time, keep your mouth shut. You don't have to like anyone, but if you irritate everyone, you won't have any sources and you'll be worthless."

"I'll behave myself."

Morrow stared at him, hating the smug look on his face. Too many of her fellow journalists seemed to be know it alls. They learned a few key phrases, a few words, and suddenly they were experts in the field. Didn't matter what the field was or how complex it was. From nuclear physics down to sewer maintenance, they knew it all. And Danforth would fit right in with them.

She picked up her camera bag, shouldered it and opened the door again. "Let's go. And I'll do the talking."

"Whatever you say, Robin."

"IF YOU'RE THROUGH with the jokes and the threats," said Maxwell, "I think we should get on with it."

"Cross-border operations are illegal," said Gerber.

"You're getting tiresome," said Maxwell.

"Okay," said Gerber. "What guarantees do Sergeant Fetterman and I have that this thing isn't going to come back on us like the last one did?"

"First," said Maxwell, "the orders are coming down the pipe to you. The last time you initiated the plan and then asked for it to be sanctioned."

"Good."

"Second, you're going after a Cambodian officer who's a thorn, not only in the side of the Saigon government, but also in that of the Cambodians. There will be no one around to complain except the North Vietnamese."

"Fine."

"And third, the target is a minor official of no real importance except for the location of his camp and his attitudes toward the South Vietnamese. His strength is that he rules with an iron hand. Once he's eliminated, his power base will erode and his men will disperse."

Gerber looked at Fetterman. "Tony?"

"Where's his camp?" the master sergeant asked.

"No more than ten klicks into Cambodia. He rarely leaves it. We're talking about an operation that will take two, three days at the very most."

"How is the change of command going to affect this?" asked Gerber.

"What do you mean?"

"Abrams isn't a fan of Special Forces or unconventional warfare. He's not going to be thrilled to learn that members of his staff have sanctioned an assassination, especially one in Cambodia."

"Change of command isn't scheduled for another week. You've got plenty of time to get into the field, accomplish your mission and get back. Westmoreland will still be in command."

"Jerry, why are you rushing this?"

Maxwell leaned forward and lowered his voice. "The North Vietnamese want to begin another push into the South. They weren't very successful with the last, except in the American press. They think that if they can create another paper storm like the last one, public opinion might force the Americans to pull out."

"And we're going to stop this?" asked Fetterman.

"We'll be taking out a staging area for the enemy, and it might be enough to inhibit the troop buildup, if only for a short time. But any problems we create will only benefit our cause."

Gerber nodded, but knew Maxwell was handing him a line. There would be other assassination teams out, or the assassination would be the cover for the real mission, a diversion so that the enemy would look in another direction while some CIA agents worked in relative safety.

"What I want to know," said Gerber, "is how you're going to protect us from our own people if the mission blows up in our faces."

"There's nothing wrong with sniper squads," Maxwell said. "The Marines employ them all the time. Each Marine division has a number of snipers assigned to it."

"But those men are used carefully, and they're not sent out against people in neutral countries. It's a completely different situation."

"The point," the CIA man pressed, "is that a sniper shooting a general isn't outside the normal operating parameters of a regular line unit. You agree?"

"I agree the Marines are using snipers," said Gerber.

"And you agree that the assignment isn't that unusual?"

Gerber thought about that for a moment. Snipers had been used in almost every war ever fought. A single well-placed round could turn the tide of a battle. Losing the general, the king, the prince was enough to crush the morale of one side, handing victory to the other. There was nothing wrong with using snipers. It was a military tradition. Gerber just wasn't sure this was the place to do it, especially with the track record the CIA had. They'd turn in their mothers if the job demanded it. Gerber glanced at Fetterman. The master sergeant shrugged, telling the captain that he didn't have a simple answer. "All right," said Gerber suddenly.

"You'll take the assignment?" Maxwell asked eagerly.

"Yes, we'll do it," said Gerber. "We won't like it, but we'll do it."

"Fine. Now, I've got a security squad lined up for you."

"Nope. We'll select our own," said Gerber. "And I'll want one of those new sniper rifles the Marines are using. The Winchester Model 79, not the XM-21, which is standard Army issue."

"Any special reason for that?" asked Maxwell.

"The bolt-action Winchester is more accurate. I won't have the urge to just jerk the trigger as I might with the M-14."

"Done."

Gerber fell back in his chair and closed his eyes for a moment. "I'll have to zero the weapon."

"There's no time for that," said Maxwell.

"Then there's no time for the mission. Listen, you can hand me an M-16 and send me on patrol without an opportunity to zero it because the odds are we'll be firing short distances without really aiming. Point and shoot. Burn through the ammo and reload quickly. But this is different. We want to take out a target from a thousand meters. At that range the slightest miscalculation will mean a miss."

Maxwell nodded, conceding the point, then turned and opened the center drawer of his desk. He pulled out a thick manila envelope and handed it to Gerber. "That contains all the information you'll need. Statistics on your target. Photos of him and a map of his camp, including the location in Cambodia. You'll need to study it and then destroy it when you're finished. Burn it.''

Gerber accepted the envelope and opened it, pulling out the picture. He looked at the man, then showed it to Fetterman, who nodded. Gerber put the picture away and took out the map.

"You can go over that later," said Maxwell.

"What if we have questions?"

"There won't be any questions. Everything you need is contained in the briefing package."

Gerber ignored Maxwell and checked the material quickly. He showed some of it to Fetterman.

Maxwell folded his hands, then nodded. "You run this your own way then."

"I plan on it," said Gerber.

Maxwell started to speak, then stopped. He let Gerber check all the material. When Gerber finally stuffed everything back into the envelope, Maxwell said, "You have everything you want?"

"I think so."

Maxwell looked at his watch. "There isn't a lot of time."

"Then," said Gerber, standing, "I think we'd better get to work on it. We'll put together our security force. We'll have them assigned to the SOG so that we can be ready to move at once. I assume you can get us aviation support."

"Choppers on standby," said Maxwell.

"We'll want to be put down as close to the border as possible. We'll want to be picked up immediately, too. I don't suppose you can get them to pluck us out of Cambodia."

Maxwell shook his head. "Not unless you really step into some deep shit. And if that happens, any American pilot will try to help you."

"We'll be in touch," said Gerber. "You find out anything about those VC who fired on us as we came out of the field?"

For a moment Maxwell was quiet, then said, "Oh, yeah. Guns tore them up and the legs moved in. Fifteen dead near the hootches and half a dozen blood trails. Grunts followed some of them, found the bodies, but then it got dark, so they moved out."

"Not too bad," said Fetterman.

Maxwell pointed at the package that Gerber held. "That man has to die within the week. Two days would be better."

"Understood," said Gerber.

Fetterman moved to the door and opened it. Gerber exited, followed by the master sergeant. As he closed the door, he said, "Just what in hell is going on here? Assassinations in Cambodia?"

Gerber shrugged. "You didn't buy that claptrap about assisting the South Vietnamese and removing a thorn from all our sides?"

"Of course not," said Fetterman. "Some local yokel in Cambodia isn't going to be that big a menace, no matter what he says or does."

"Do you want to back out of this mission?" asked Gerber.

"No, sir. I just want it understood that I'm not so dense that I can't see through the cover. Maxwell was handing us a line, and we both know it."

"Of course," agreed Gerber, "but then the mission isn't that far out of line with what we've done in the past. A walk in the woods, some target practice and we come on home."

"Yes, sir. Sounds easy."

Gerber agreed with that, too, and that was what scared him. It sounded way too easy.

MAXWELL SAT in his office until he was sure Gerber and Fetterman had had time to clear the building. He then put the classified material in the safe, locked it and left his office. Like everyone else, he signed out at the gate.

Upstairs, he turned right and walked down a hallway, passing men in jungle fatigues and khakis and Vietnamese women in skirts and blouses and light dresses. He ignored all of them, along with the posters on the walls.

Coming to a closed door, he tapped once, then opened it and stepped into the outer office. An armed MP sat in a chair in the corner, a pump shotgun across his knees in the manner of a bank guard of the Old West. With bored eyes he glanced at Maxwell, then settled back.

Maxwell moved to the desk in front of him where a major sat quietly. "Yes?" he asked the CIA man.

"Is he in?"

"In a meeting."

Maxwell turned and looked at the couch pushed against the wall. A coffee table, covered with magazines and newspapers, sat in front of it. A ceiling fan stirred the air.

He stood there for a moment, then decided he didn't want to see Hansen now. The general would be of no help to him, and he could let him know later that the first of the teams was going out. There were more important things to do. "Tell the general I'll be around this afternoon to brief him on the operation."

The major nodded. "Of course."

Maxwell left the office and hurried from the building. At the double doors he stopped, making sure that neither Gerber nor Fetterman was visible. He then stepped out into the blast furnace of the late morning and rushed down the sidewalk to the parking lot where his jeep stood waiting.

He climbed in and used his key to unfasten the padlock and chain wrapped around the steering wheel. Twisting in the seat so that he could check the traffic, he saw a break in the line of vehicles and pulled out.

The drive to the American embassy was short. Maxwell weaved in and out of the traffic, taking almost no notice of it. He glanced over his shoulder once or twice, looking for a tail, but spotted nothing. Still, he was aware that in Saigon he could be followed on a bicycle or in a car, or by radio as one man on the roof radioed another. Besides, he was on his way to the embassy, which meant nothing by itself, so it really didn't matter anyway.

He was stopped at the gate until the Marine guards identified him. Then he was allowed in and told to park the jeep at the rear of the building, out of the way.

It wasn't first-class treatment, but then he didn't mind. The VC agents who watched the gate all the time would just write down that some minor official had arrived. He wasn't important enough for anyone to notice or try to name. Just a guy in a jeep who had to identify himself at the gate. He wouldn't become a target that way.

Inside, he was ignored by everyone. He made his way to the rear, up a flight of stairs and down a brightly lit corridor. The tile on the floor was light gray and the walls were painted off-white. Pictures, scenes of Saigon and Vietnam, were hung at intervals. In a few places the solid walls had been replaced by glass so that those in the hall could see into the offices. Maxwell passed one that had four female secretaries typing away. A short-haired blonde glanced at him and smiled.

At the far end he found a steel door with a combination lock in place of the knob. He knocked on it. The door rung with the sound. A moment later a small eye-level window was opened and an eye appeared. The little door closed immediately.

Maxwell didn't move. There was sound from inside and the big door opened. Without waiting for an invitation,

Maxwell entered. Once he was inside the door was shut and locked.

It was like stepping into a brightly lit vault. Gray carpeting covered the floor and the walls were made of metal. There was a single battleship-gray desk that looked as if it had been delivered that morning. A plush chair with a cloth seat and back was behind it. On one side were metal bookcases, holding various volumes. Near the desk on the other side was a shredder that fed directly into a fifty-five-gallon drum. There were also thermite grenades on the bookshelves in case there wasn't time to shred everything.

Behind the desk was a window that looked into another room. A small conference table, six chairs, more bookcases and a few filing cabinets comprised the contents of the second room. There was a single person there.

Maxwell walked in and sat at the table. The other occupant joined him, pulling her chair around. Maxwell stared into her cold blue eyes and discovered there was nothing in them. No fire, no emotion. Nothing. They were as dead and as cold as the bottom of the ocean. Barren. Lifeless.

And yet the woman was beautiful. Dark hair brushed her eyebrows. She had delicate, perfect features, flawless white teeth, an hourglass figure that she did nothing to conceal and legs that were the most shapely he'd ever seen.

"You have a reason to be here?" she asked in a voice dripping with sexuality.

"Yes, Margarite, I do."

"Give it to me."

He studied her for a moment. Some of her background had been explained to him. Once she had been the top CIA assassin. Cold and heartless, she used her beauty to trap her victims, both men and women. It was surprising how many women succumbed to her. But it had done something to her, wiped out her feelings and her heart, and now she cared about nothing except the mission.

"Gerber and Fetterman have been dispatched on the first step. They'll kill Kong Samphan within the next two or three days."

"And your man?"

"Is ready now. He's already planted the seeds of dissent with the troops. When Samphan falls, our man will leap forward to take command."

"And your assassins?"

"They'll make their way back to South Vietnam."

"No," she said. "You'll have your man lead his soldiers in pursuit. They'll hunt down and kill the assassins. One more proof of his strength and power."

Maxwell sat there quietly, digesting the information. "That might not be a smart move."

"Your man will be given the escape route of the assassins. It'll be no problem to hunt them down and kill them."

Maxwell was suddenly nervous. He rubbed his face and shifted around in his chair. He glanced to the rear, through the window, and saw two men working in the other room. He lifted a hand and pulled at his lips. "I wish I'd known about this sooner."

"Why? So that you could alert your Army friends?"

"No," said Maxwell. "So that I could have chosen a different team. Gerber and Fetterman won't be stopped easily. Our man will lose quite a few of his people if we force him to proceed like this."

"Then his victory will be even more glorious."

"I must protest," said Maxwell.

"Protest all you want," she said. "Protest to everyone you can find. But the orders are given. Phoenix must proceed at all costs."

"At all costs."

She smiled at him then and leaned closer. Touching his hand, she let him peek down the top of her dress, a glance to take his mind off the orders she had given him. "There's no problem, is there?"

"No," said Maxwell. "No problem." He stood and backed up to the door. She swung around so that he could see her legs, crossing them slowly, showing him her thighs all the way to the crotch.

Maxwell turned and fumbled for the door handle. He felt sweat break out on his face. His underarms were clammy. There was an aura about her, a power he didn't understand, but which drew him in anyway, a magic ability that would make him agree to anything just so that she would smile at him.

He stumbled out of the conference room, then glanced back through the window. She sat there as if frozen, staring at him.

Without a word, he moved to the door and then waited as one of the men opened it. As he moved, the man whispered, "She's one cold bitch."

"But beautiful."

"Oh, God, is she ever."

Maxwell stepped into the hallway, and when the vault door closed behind him, he fell back against the wall. He dug out his handkerchief from his pocket and mopped his face. Closing his eyes, he tried to get his breath back, tried hard to suck the artificially cool air into his lungs so that he could breathe again, think once more.

"Phoenix must not fail," he said to himself. "Must not."

An instant later Morrow was there, looking at him. "Jerry, are you all right?"

He opened his eyes and tried to smile. "It's the damn heat. Or the humidity. Or some damn something. In and out of all these air-conditioned buildings. All day, everyday. Makes me sick sometimes.''

"You need some help?" she asked.

Maxwell forced himself to straighten, then remembered what Margarite had said and who she had been talking about. He stared at Morrow and shook his head. "I'm fine," he said. "Just fine." He started down the hall toward the stairs.

He didn't hear Danforth turn to Morrow and ask, "What's Phoenix?"

9

THE SOG BUILDING TAN
SON NHUT

After the delivery of the sniper rifle, Gerber spent the remainder of the morning on the range carefully zeroing it. He used targets at two hundred meters, then five hundred and finally one thousand meters. He put enough rounds through the weapon so that he understood it as he adjusted it to his own body dimensions. Each man would have a different grip on the weapon, depending on the size of his hands, the length of his arms and the construction of his shoulder. Each man would use the scope differently, and all those variables could make a long shot miss, unless the weapon had been zeroed for that particular individual.

Now, with the weapon safely encased in a specially designed pouch, with the scope carefully and tightly attached to the rifle, he was ready. The team, the security men who would make sure no one surprised him as he set up for and then attempted to make the shot, had yet to be picked.

Fetterman sat in the tiny conference room of the SOG building, looking over the records of the men available at that moment in Saigon, either on leave, pass or permanently assigned to MACV-SOG.

"I think we can put together a good team," said Fetterman, looking up as Gerber entered.

"No more than five," said Gerber. He closed the door behind him, locking it so that they wouldn't be disturbed.

"I'd take Tyson and Braver, only because they're here and we just worked with them."

"No objections. And what about that striker NCO, Sergeant Thai? He might be valuable."

"I was thinking about keeping this an all-American operation."

"There a reason for that?" asked Gerber.

"No, sir. I just thought a cross-border operation might go smoother with Americans."

"Hell, it'd go smoother with no Americans at all," said Gerber.

"Except that we've been ordered to make the shot."

"Except for that." He moved around the table so that he could sit facing the door, then he pulled the envelope that Maxwell had given him closer and sat down.

"Do you want Thai with us?" asked Fetterman.

"I think he'd be an asset."

"Then we only need two others for the security team. I'd like to find Kepler and use him."

"Why?"

"Just his intelligence background," said Fetterman. "He might see things that we'd miss."

"I have no objections to Derek."

"There's a sergeant here named Reese who could fill in the last slot. He's on his second tour."

"Then get him," said Gerber. He opened the envelope and pulled out the briefing packet. On top was a black-and-white glossy print of their target. It appeared to have been taken with a telephoto lens from a long distance, and Gerber idly wondered why the photographer couldn't have picked him off. It would have saved them a trek through the jungle.

He put the picture on the table and looked at the report that accompanied it. There wasn't much, other than a sketchy background of the man and a list of suspected meetings with the North Vietnamese. There was also a second photograph, showing the target surrounded by his men, all of them holding AKs.

The last thing was a map showing the location of the target's camp. Not far into Cambodia, just across the border. Easy walking distance for the assassination team.

Fetterman finished with the records, stood and came around to stand behind Gerber. He stared down at the picture of the target. A dark-skinned Cambodian in a fancy uniform stood in front of a mud-and-thatch hootch. "Doesn't look like much," the master sergeant grumbled.

"Napolean was what, five-two? And he started a war that involved most of Europe."

"This guy doesn't have the power base to work from."

Gerber dropped the documents onto the table and turned to stare up at Fetterman. "That's what bothers me about this whole deal. He doesn't have a power base, yet he's targeted. Seems like a waste of our talents to take this clown out."

Fetterman sat on the edge of the table and twisted the picture around to study it. He then pulled the second one forward, placing it right next to the first. "Maybe he's like Hitler. Kind of a joke, and the next thing you know he's got the power. If the North Vietnamese are courting the guy, maybe they know something we don't."

Gerber picked up the picture again. "Maybe."

DANFORTH WAS QUIET on the way back to the office. He held his tongue in the cab, even though he was bursting to ask questions. He kept quiet, not because he was afraid the driver might be VC, but because he was afraid the man might be on the payroll of a rival news organization. It happened all the time—rival reporters bribing taxi drivers, bellhops and waitresses to listen and report. The last thing he wanted was to hand the real enemy in Vietnam a hot story. Danforth considered the network people, the news magazine reporters and the foreign press to be the real enemy.

Once they reached the building and began to climb the stairs to the second floor, he couldn't contain himself any longer. "Who was that Maxwell guy?"

"Civilian who works over at MACV."

"As what? He the CIA guy?"

Morrow stopped at the top of the stairs. "That's an area where we don't speculate."

"Why?" His voice took on a mocking tone. "Afraid of burning another source?"

"Not at all, fathead," she said sweetly. "We don't speculate about it because we don't want the VC to pick up our suspicions about people."

"Why not? If he's CIA, he deserves to be burned."

"Christ," said Morrow, "who died and left you in charge? How do you know he deserves to be burned?"

"He's CIA."

"I never said that. You said that. I told you he was a civilian employee at MACV. There are a number of them, and they're not all CIA."

"And I'll wager that most, if not all, are on the CIA payroll in some capacity."

"Probably."

They started down the hallway. As they reached the doors to the city room, Danforth asked. "What's this Phoenix?"

"Now that's a good question," said Morrow. "I haven't heard that before."

"So how do we find out?"

"Well, we don't go over to MACV and ask. If we do, they'll all pretend they've never heard of it. What we do is pretend that we know and let them talk about it."

They entered the city room and headed toward the front. Morrow put her camera bag on her desk, glanced at the messages stacked there and sorted through them quickly. Then she dropped into her chair.

"The phoenix," said Danforth, "was the mythical bird that rose from its own ashes. Maybe the name has something to do with that."

"Phoenix is also the capital of Arizona," she said idly. "Besides, code names rarely have any relevance to what they're about. If they did that, some bright reporter might figure it out."

"So what are we going to do about this?"

Morrow started sorting through her messages again. "Do about what?"

"Finding out what Maxwell does over at MACV and what this Phoenix is."

"Those sound like good projects for you," said Morrow. "I've shown you around. You can find a cab for yourself, we got your press credentials at the embassy, got you your ID card. I don't know what more I can do for you."

"You're giving me the story?"

"What story? We overheard a single word that could mean absolutely nothing, except to the people of Arizona." She held up a hand. "I'll give you one more bit of advice. Don't go over to MACV and ask if Maxwell is CIA."

"Why not?"

"Because you'll end up looking like a jerk and no one will talk to you. Use some finesse."

Danforth stood there for a moment. "I really appreciate your doing this for me."

"What?"

"Letting me check on the stories. Letting me have the leads we developed together."

Morrow laughed. "There are no leads and there is no story. But if you want to run off on this wild-goose chase, you go right ahead."

"Well, thanks anyway."

Morrow watched as Danforth turned and headed back toward the door. He pushed on through and disappeared. As he did, Hodges came out of his glass cubicle and walked over to her. "Where's the boy wonder going?"

"Off to MACV to learn about the CIA and Phoenix."

"By himself?"

Morrow turned and looked up at Hodges. "All new pilots must solo sometime. I've done everything I care to do for him. Taught him all I know. Now the only thing left is for him to crash and burn."

"I hope it's not too bloody," said Hodges.

"I hope it is," muttered Morrow.

MAXWELL SAT IN HIS OFFICE and tried to read the latest reports on the number of VC and NVA operating in the Three Corps Tactical Area. He read the report twice and still had no idea what it said. After his meeting with Margarite, he had no concentration left.

He stood up and walked around his office, touching things, as if to ascertain their reality. The filing cabinets, hard and cold. The cinder block of the walls and the vinyl of the overused visitor's chair. All real.

As was his assignment.

He flopped down in the visitor's chair, closed his eyes and let his mind drift. Of course Margarite was right. Assassinating Samphan wouldn't be enough. His man in the field would have to make a grandstand play of finding and killing the assassins. That would certainly cement his place at the top of the power structure. It would enable him to move higher and put him in a position to take over other units as their leaders died or were assassinated. Eventually all the small military units would be combined into a single fighting force that could withstand both pressure from the North Vietnamese and the army of the Cambodian government.

It was an ambitious plan—no doubt about it. But if it worked, then the thorn of Cambodia would be removed from the side of American forces in South Vietnam. A strong Cambodia would prop up a weaker South Vietnam, keeping the Communists at bay in the North, and keep them away from Thailand. That was the plan, pure and simple.

And Maxwell was certain it could work. If it didn't, then no one was the wiser, but even in failure it would succeed in part. Cambodian leaders who favored the Communists would be dead, replaced by those who looked to the West for economic and military support. The situation would be better than it was now.

Again he was up and walking around. It was Gerber and Fetterman that bothered him. These were men he knew. Men he counted among the few friends he had. Now they were to be sacrificed so that a plan could come to fruition two or three years down the road.

That was the trouble with making friends. You didn't know when you were going to have to turn against them. Like now. He'd told them the mission was sanctioned by the Army, and it was. But he'd also told them that there would be aviation support for them, even in Cambodia, if they stepped in it. Now that might be turned into a lie.

Maxwell had learned his lesson before. He had sent Gerber and Fetterman out on missions where there were supposed to be no survivors, so he hadn't bothered with arranging for pickup. The men survived and came looking for him. A sticky situation.

The solution was obvious. Arrange the support but deny permission for the choppers to operate cross-border. Nothing wrong with that. It followed guidelines, and Maxwell could always blame the bureaucrats in Saigon who were ruining the war for everyone.

"Yes," he said out loud. He liked that. Kept him clear and maintained the fiction that he was a good and trustworthy man. Gerber couldn't blame him if the aviation units were required to stay on the Vietnamese side of the border.

But that didn't get around the other problem. Alerting the Cambodians so that they would be in a position to exploit the death of Samphan. That was something that had to be done on the sly. The majority of the Cambodians had to be kept in the dark so that they would follow the new leader, and Gerber and Fetterman had to be kept in the dark so that they would play their roles out to the very end.

This was what Maxwell didn't like—having information that could keep his friends alive, but being forbidden to pass it on to them. The right word, a cautious word, and Gerber and Fetterman would understand the whole plan. They could plan for the sudden attacks on them after the shot was fired.

For a moment he considered it. See them at the SOG building and suggest they watch for a swift response to the shot. And then he put the thought out of his mind. There would be no warning, even to friends, because the mission came first. The mission always came first. After it was accomplished, everyone who survived could sit around and talk about it, but not until then. Sometimes there were secrets that had to be kept.

Maxwell decided he wouldn't be able to concentrate on the reports, so he gathered them up and stuffed them back into his safe. Closing and locking it, he then checked the office quickly, making sure there was nothing classified left out.

Again he signed out and again he walked out into the bright sunlight and the heat of the Saigon day. He got behind the wheel of his jeep, unlocked it and headed out toward Tan Son Nhut. The drive passed without him seeing much of it. He was barely aware of the other traffic around him. The sights and smells were missing as his mind raced.

He was almost stopped at the gate, but the AP saw an American driving the jeep and waved him through. Without thinking about it, he drove to the Air America hangar. Pulling up beside the building, he didn't see the three DC-3s, painted white, blue and silver that sat on the ramp in front. Nor did he see the two Huey helicopters.

He entered a side door and walked across the open hangar floor where two more Hueys sat. Three men worked on one, the turbine exposed. One of them stood on yellow scaffolding that seemed to grow from the side of the aircraft.

Maxwell walked to a side door and then used the stairs to climb to the second floor. He walked down the poorly lit hallway, noting the offices off to the right. A few of them stood open, and he could see desks inside. Men and women worked at them, but none of them were Vietnamese.

At the end of the hallway he opened a door and stepped into a small alcove. There were more doors on the other three sides. He continued on into a large room that was cut in half by a console. There were radios built into the console, and men in civilian clothes worked them. The room also contained a scheduling board filled with black grease pencil notations, an acetate map of Vietnam on one wall and a small window that looked out onto the airfield.

One of the civilians turned. "You need something, Jerry?"

"A ride out into the boonies this afternoon. I need to rendezvous with one of my agents."

The man, a big brute who looked as if he'd played football longer ago than he'd probably care to admit, spun. He had sandy-colored hair, fleshy features and a double chin. He needed a shave, and judging by the sweat stains on his shirt, a bath. "You want one of ours or Army Aviation's?"

"Going into Cambodia."

"One of ours then." He glanced at Maxwell. "You going to wear that suit?"

"I'm going down and draw some fatigues."

"You going to want anyone with you?"

"Nope. In and out. Couple of hours. I'll need to use the radio room to set up the meet and then I'll have the full schedule."

"Guns?" asked the man, pulling a clipboard closer.

"Be nice if there were a couple of fighters and helicopter gunships standing by. On the South Vietnamese side of the border."

"You got it. Anything else?"

"That'll do, I think. Just a quick in-and-out operation to set up a couple of other things."

"I'll get this arranged. As soon as you have your end figured, you let me know so that I can get going."

"We have a problem with scheduling?"

"Nope. Right now everything is quiet. You want, I can get you a regiment of Thai or Cambode strikers."

"No thanks," said Maxwell. But he was happy to hear that everything was quiet. It would mean that the chances of anything going wrong on his trip were greatly reduced. He moved back to the door. "I'll be back here as quick as I can make it."

"Right," said the big man, but he was already more interested in his radios.

10

SOG BUILDING TAN SON NHUT

The helicopters from the Army's 116th Assault Helicopter company sat on the pad in front of the SOG building, their rotors spinning and their turbines roaring. With the pitch of the blades leveled, they weren't creating the normal whirlwind of dust and debris. Now they just made noise.

Gerber stood inside the building, aware that the choppers had landed five minutes earlier. Everyone was aware of it. Fetterman, standing at the rear of the room, Tyson, Braver, Thai and Kepler were all aware of it. Reese, it turned out, wasn't available.

Gerber had greeted Kepler when he'd arrived about thirty minutes earlier. Kepler had been with Gerber on his first tour, as the intel NCO. He was a large man with short dark hair and a talent for finding the things they needed—a scrounger. He also tended to dress in costume, once portraying a Navy lieutenant commander when they'd needed a small speedboat. But he'd never explained why he'd shown up at the camp once, dressed as an Army nurse, down to the underwear and combat boots.

When everyone was present, Gerber gave them the mission details. A quick in-and-out job. He, working with Fetterman, would be the sniper and spotter. The rest, under the direction of Sergeant Kepler, would make up the security team. Their job was to kill one officer, then get out. Nothing fancy. They could ride to the border, walk for the rest of the day and be into position about dusk with a little luck.

"I'll make the shot first chance I get. Then we're out of there."

"Might be better to wait until dark before moving in," suggested Kepler.

"Not with the border as close as it is. We'll only be an hour or two from safety. Best to get it done and get out as quickly as possible."

"If we make contact?" asked Braver.

"We break it as quickly as possible. Basic load of grenades, smoke, CS and fragmentation for everyone. We're not there to chop up the enemy or to make contact. We do our job and get the hell out."

After that they talked about the equipment they would need—food, water, bandoliers of ammo, insect repellent, combat knives and first-aid kits. All the men had brought their own gear with them. From the supplies kept in the rear of the SOG building, they drew whatever else they needed, included a hand-held URC-10 for each of them, and the AN/PRR9 and the AN/PRT4 for intrasquad communications.

Aware that the choppers were still on the ramp and still burning JP-4, Gerber said, "If we get separated, make tracks due east. That'll put you back into South Vietnam quickly. Then it's up to each of you to arrange a trip back to Saigon."

Fetterman added, "Once the shot is made, the captain and I will try to link up. If we fail, then you'll have to make your own way out. Everyone understand?"

Kepler nodded. "Who's got command of security?"

"You, of course, Derek," said Gerber.

"Fine."

Gerber turned toward the wall, but there was no window that would allow him to see the choppers. "There's no time for a proper briefing, but then all you have to know is how to run security. No one approaches us for any reason once we're in place."

"Got it, Captain," Kepler said.

"Then let's go." Gerber bent down and shouldered his pack. He picked up the case holding the Winchester carefully. Fetterman had a spare M-16 in the event Gerber wanted or needed it. Both of them carried Browning M-35 pistols. Kepler had brought along a silenced .22.

Gerber moved to the door, hesitated, then looked back. The others were on their feet, moving toward him. He opened the door and stepped out into the sweltering afternoon. The air smelled of burning aviation gas and diesel oil. Ducking, Gerber hurried to the lead chopper, leaped into the rear and crawled up to the console.

"You Gerber?" shouted the aircraft commander.

"I'm Gerber."

The pilot pulled a map across his lap and dropped it onto the console. "Where do you want to go?"

Gerber stabbed a finger at the spot. "Here. Anywhere around here. That a problem?"

"Nope."

Gerber slipped to the rear and sat down on the troop seat. Fetterman joined him. The others climbed into the second aircraft. There was no one for the third. He'd be back there, lending moral support if they found they needed it, an added element to confuse the enemy.

Just as Gerber sat down, the helicopter lifted, hovered closer to the runways, then took off, climbing out over the active. They continued south, connected with Highway One, then turned west, leveling off at fifteen hundred feet.

They followed the highway until they reached Go Dau Ha, a small town that Gerber recognized by the bridge and the river. He'd heard a pilot say he'd never seen the span across the water. It seemed that every time he got to Go Dau Ha the bridge was down, the twisted wreckage in the water. There were bunkers on either side of the road and on either side of the river, but they didn't do any good. American engineers would erect a new bridge and VC sappers would quickly knock it down.

They crossed the river, then stayed on the northern side, flying more or less toward Tay Ninh, a city of more than a million people. To the northwest there was a big American base, while a small Special Forces camp lay due north. With choppers, help wouldn't be more than twenty minutes away, if they needed it.

As they continued north of Tay Ninh, the nature of the land changed. Where previously it had been light forest north of the highway and swamp to the south, with thick pockets of jungle, several small villages and a couple of American fire support bases, now the forests became jungles, initially single canopy, but then eventually very dense triple canopy.

The crew chief leaned around the transmission wall and shouted, "We're getting close. Any last instructions?"

"Just hit an LZ and then get the hell out. You receive any fire, ignore it. We'll take care of the problem."

"Yes, sir."

Gerber touched Fetterman on the shoulder. The master sergeant nodded his understanding. Ahead, through the windshield, Gerber could see the circle that marked the LZ— a break in the otherwise thick green sea.

"Here we go!" shouted Fetterman over the roar of the engine and the pop of the rotors.

Gerber slipped from the troop seat to one knee, crouching in the cargo compartment doorway of the chopper. He held the Winchester in both hands because he didn't want to jar it. That could throw the optics off.

Under him the jungle canopy rushed by in a thick green blur. He turned his head and glanced through the windshield again. They were getting closer and lower. Off to the right were two gunships, escorts that had been picked up somewhere after they had passed Tay Ninh.

Maxwell had come through for them. He'd arranged for Army Aviation to pick them up, then arranged for gunship support. If they needed the guns, they would have to abort the mission, but it was nice to know the support was available if they stepped into it deeply.

The crew chief, now sitting behind his M-60 machine gun, yelled, "About thirty seconds!"

A moment later the bottom dropped out. Gerber felt himself rising slightly as he became weightless. He grabbed at the rear of the pilot's armor seat and was forced down as the aircraft flared, the ground rushing up at them. He caught a flash of green and then deep blue sky. Again the chopper dropped, there was a single, rough bounce and then they were sitting on the LZ.

Gerber leaped clear, landing in the tall grass. As he crouched, the wind from the rotors almost flattened him. The rotor wash tore at his clothes and filled the air around him with dried grass and clouds of dust. He bowed his head and closed his eyes.

As one, the three helicopters lifted off. As they did, there was a single burst of AK fire, somewhere to the north. Gerber dived for the ground but kept his head up, trying to spot the enemy weapon.

An instant later, as the noise from the choppers faded, Fetterman knelt next to him. "You see where it came from?"

Gerber climbed to his knees. "Nope."

"Then we'd better hurry."

Kepler was right there with them, his M-16 clutched in his hands, boonie hat pulled low. "You see where that firing came from?"

"North of here," said Gerber. "But I didn't see anything."

"Should we go after him?"

Gerber shook his head and then quickly changed his mind. "We'd better make the effort. Derek, get the men moving."

Kepler waved a hand and began trotting toward the trees. He kept his head up and moving, searching for a sign of the enemy soldier.

As he entered the trees, Gerber started to move, following the path Kepler had taken. Fetterman was right behind him. They reached the trees and split up. Gerber slipped to one knee and stared into the gloom of the triple-canopy jungle. Now that the choppers were gone, the natural noises began to swell. Birds and monkeys and lizards and cats. Quiet trilling from insects and an insistent buzz, along with the persistent dripping of water working its way from the upper level down to the ground. It could rain overhead and they wouldn't know it for an hour, since it would take that long for the water to seep through the triple canopy.

"How long?" asked Fetterman.

"No more than an hour," said Gerber. He slung the Winchester over his shoulder and then took the spare M-16 from Fetterman.

Using his compass, he oriented himself and then stopped moving. He listened carefully but couldn't hear any sounds that suggested there were other people around.

There was a quiet burst from the intrasquad radio and then Kepler's whispered voice came through. "We've got him spotted. One man with an AK. Do we take him?"

Without hesitation Gerber said, "Roger."

A moment later there was a single shot—an M-16—and then silence again.

"Kepler got him," said Fetterman.

"Got him damn quick," Gerber agreed.

"No reason for him to be out here. Shouldn't have shot at the choppers."

Gerber nodded, then took out his map. If they'd gotten the LZ right, and there was no reason to assume they hadn't, it was two, three hours to the Cambodian camp. There were a number of small streams to cross, but no major rivers. They could avoid the swamp and stick to the jungle.

Satisfied he knew where they were and what was going on, Gerber folded the map and stuck it into his pocket. Then he took a final compass reading and waited.

When Kepler appeared, he was carrying an AK-47, a chest pouch and a pistol belt. "One guy," he said. "One old guy. I don't know what he thought he was doing."

"Fine," said Gerber. "Tony, you take point. Derek, you've got the rear. Questions?"

There were none. Fetterman moved out and the patrol fell in behind him, moving west.

MAXWELL WAS WEARING new jungle fatigues with no insignia on them and a pistol belt that held a single canteen. He also carried a CAR-15. Leaving the hangar, he walked over to one of the Air America Hueys parked next to the DC-3s. There were four civilians sitting on the ground near the chopper. They were playing cards. The pot was considerable and contained several gold trinkets. The gold was what the pilots used to buy their way to freedom if they found themselves downed anywhere in Southeast Asia. Gold went a long way with the locals.

As Maxwell arrived, one of the men laughed, glanced upward as if thanking the gods and raked in the dough. "Gentlemen, you have made the little lady very happy."

"Which little lady might that be, Brad?" asked a dark-haired man who wore mirrored sunglasses.

"Nan or Fran or whatever the hell her name is. I get back to Bangkok and we're going to have some kind of party. When I arrive, she only has one goal—please me."

"Until the money runs out."

Brad laughed again. "But with you patsies around, I'm not going to have to worry about that."

Maxwell stepped up to them. "Who's going to fly me out to my meeting?"

The man in the mirrored glasses stood up. He was very tall, at least six-four, but skinny. His khaki shirt was sweat-soaked and his blue jeans were covered with grease. He had a bushy mustache and long, flowing hair. The mustache drew Maxwell's attention.

"That'd be me. You ready?"

"I'm set, though I hate to drag you away from the game."

"Shit, that's fine. Brad's having himself a day, and I'd like an excuse to get out of here before he gets the rest of my dough."

Another civilian stood and opened the closed cargo compartment door. He stood next to it, arms folded across his chest. He had massive forearms and both wrists were banded by thick gold bracelets. Maxwell looked up, into his face, but the features were bland. He was average-looking, except for his red hair and freckles. "I've got a date tonight," he told Maxwell.

The CIA man nodded. "I'll do everything in my power to get through early enough for you to make your date."

"You don't understand. This is with a round eye. A nurse or something. And she wants it bad."

Maxwell pushed past the man and climbed into the rear of the helicopter. "Then let's get going."

"He's got you there, Chuck." The man with the mirrored glasses stuck out a hand. "Call me Andy."

"Fine, Andy. I'm ready. You know the drill?"

"Map coordinates are all I need."

Maxwell took out his map, opened it and pointed. "Right about there. Narrow road, but enough room to put down. Hootch to the right. Our people will be in it."

"I wait on the ground or take off?"

"On the ground. I'll be no more than five minutes. Longer than that and you can get out, if you can. Longer than that and it's an ambush."

"Got it."

Andy turned and pulled the cargo compartment door shut. He then opened the cockpit door, climbed in and buckled up. Reaching for a headset, which hung slightly behind his head, he put it on and adjusted the boom mike so that it was in front of his lips.

Chuck climbed in the other side and did the same. He then began flipping switches, setting the controls and getting ready to start the turbine.

Maxwell sat there, baking in the rapidly heating interior of the closed chopper. The sun beat down, blistering the metal of the helicopter. Sweat poured from him, soaking his new fatigues, turning them black under the arms and down the back. He tugged at the pistol belt that held his canteen, a small first-aid kit and a pistol, then wiped his forehead on the right sleeve of his uniform.

The turbine began to whine, a low sound that quickly built to a roar. The rotor began to spin, slow at first, and then faster and faster until it was little more than a blur, the blades popping in the heat of the afternoon.

In a minute they were airborne, hovering above the white-hot tarmac, the brightness of the airfield nearly blinding Maxwell. He held a hand up to shade his eyes, watching as a single fighter rolled down the runway and leaped into the sky. He couldn't hear the roar of its engines over that of the turbine right behind him.

Then they were on the move, across the taxiways and runways. He saw two more fighters sitting at the end of the runway, waiting their turn for departure. He was pressed back against the gray soundproofing of the transmission wall as the pilot hauled back on the cyclic and climbed rapidly.

They reached fifteen hundred feet and passed through it, climbing to five thousand, where the air was cooler and they wouldn't be as noticeable to people on the ground.

Now it was cool in the chopper. Maxwell felt better with the heat gone. They moved slowly, it seemed, as they cruised above the rice paddies and forests near Highway One. Crossing over Go Dau Ha, they turned gradually north and missed the big city of Tay Ninh and its American bases.

The pilot turned, and over the roar of the engine, shouted, "We're getting close to the border. We'll be low-leveling from that point."

Maxwell nodded, then closed his eyes. Low-leveling was something he hated. The aircraft would be no more than two or three feet off the ground, or just above the jungle which would put them at constant risk. It would be a wild ride, not unlike that of a roller coaster gone mad.

As the pilot turned back, the helicopter began a plunge toward the ground. Maxwell's stomach suddenly heaved. He clamped his hands on the metal rods that supported the troop seat, took a deep breath and opened his eyes. It looked as if they were diving into the center of a deep green sea. He couldn't stand it. He snapped his eyes shut and began silently singing to himself, trying to take his mind off the ride.

They bottomed out suddenly, and Maxwell thought he was going to throw up. He was forced down against the troop seat. His head hurt as the blood was forced from it. He felt a curtain of black begin to descend and then lift as they leveled off.

Again the pilot looked over the back of his seat. "About five minutes."

Maxwell opened his eyes and nodded dumbly. "Five minutes," he repeated.

They raced along the treetops, dodging and weaving to avoid those that stuck up through the canopy. They stayed close to the vegetation, and once Maxwell was sure they actually brushed through a treetop.

"Coming up on it!" yelled the pilot. This time he didn't turn around but kept his hands close to the controls, following the movements made by the aircraft commander.

Suddenly they flared, the nose of the chopper coming up, pointing into the bright blue sky. Maxwell was thrown back against the transmission wall. For a moment it seemed as if he were lying on his back like an astronaut waiting to rocket into space.

And then the chopper righted itself and leveled off. They hovered above a road, then slowly sank toward it, kicking up a cloud of red dust that obscured the surrounding jungle and the hootch off to the right.

Maxwell unbuckled his seat belt and moved to the cargo compartment door. Using the handle, he slid it open, then shouted. "I'll be no more than five minutes. You hear shooting, you get the hell out."

"Roger."

He dropped to the road, reached over and adjusted the holster of his pistol, unhooking the strap. He had little faith that he could outdraw anyone, especially a man holding an AK or M-16, but he unfastened the strap anyway. He wiped the sweat from his face, picked up the CAR-15 and walked across the road.

The hootch was a mud-and-wood structure with a rusting, corrugated tin roof. There was a porch on the front. A man in black pajamas sat on it, watching, but didn't seem concerned about the appearance of the helicopter.

Maxwell moved to the porch and stopped. He was aware of the bright sunlight, the green of the jungle only a few feet behind the hootch, the smell of dust in the air thanks to the rotor blades of the chopper, and the sound of the aircraft behind him. He looked into the brown eyes of the man sitting on the porch and realized the man was studying him just as intently.

"I'm going inside," said Maxwell.

The man said nothing and remained motionless. Maxwell walked past him and stopped in the doorway. The interior looked black until his eyes began to adjust. Inside were two men, a table and four chairs. Each of the men had a weapon, but only one of them wore a uniform.

Maxwell entered and sat down in one of the vacant chairs. He set his CAR-15 on the table near his hand and leaned forward but didn't speak.

"I have taken a major risk coming here," said the man in uniform.

"I'm aware of the risk, but you're not alone in that. I, too, am taking a major risk."

"So we are both brave men."

Maxwell nodded toward the other man. He was small and wore a dirty, sweat-stained khaki uniform. "You trust him?"

"He is my ally and he speaks no English."

Maxwell took a deep breath and blew it out. He wiped away the sweat a final time and lowered his voice. "Tomorrow or the next day at the very latest, it'll happen. The team has already been dispatched."

"And?" said the man.

"Once the shot has been made, you must find and eliminate the assassination squad."

"Why?"

"Because it'll solidify your support. It'll make you stronger when you avenge the death of your general."

"I understand."

"The men who fire the shot will come from the east and will want to retreat in that direction. Enough men thrown out should be able to catch and kill them. Make sure you kill them. We can't afford to have them talk."

"I understand."

Maxwell took a map from his pocket and put it on the table. "Everything you need to know is here. Without having seen the terrain around your camp myself, I couldn't pinpoint the exact location of the sniper team, but I've shown the general location where they'll be operating, as well as their line of march in and suspected line of retreat."

"You want me to kill these men?"

Maxwell shrugged. He felt his stomach flip over and a cold sweat break out. "Yes, it's the only way."

"I do not understand this, but it will be done."

Now Maxwell stood up. "Tomorrow or the next day. You be ready to move."

"It will be done."

Maxwell hurried to the door. The scene outside hadn't changed. He ran to the edge of the road, then walked across it. Once he was in the rear of the chopper, he shouted, "Let's get the fuck out of here!"

11

MACV HEADQUARTERS
SAIGON

For the first few minutes Danforth wandered the hallways, looking at the signs on doors and trying to figure out who might know something about Phoenix. Because he knew nothing about it, other than the name, he didn't know where to start. Finally he found an open door that led into a loungelike area.

Morrow, he knew, wouldn't have had this problem. She'd been around long enough to know who to ask. He should have asked her to come with him. But she had been sure that he was off on another tangent, and she didn't want to be seen with him again. He'd made too many enemies too quickly.

So she was out. He sat in the lounge, looking at copies of various magazines scattered on the table, and tried to think his way through the problem. Supply and personnel would be likely candidates to forget. In none of those areas would there be a need for secrets, except concerning the actual movement of equipment and weapons from one base to another.

He thought about the encounter in the hallway of the embassy and realized that the man he'd seen, Maxwell, was coming from a security area that related to intelligence. The deduction that followed was that Maxwell, if not CIA, had something to do with intelligence. Morrow didn't have to tell him that. He could see it, had seen it, for himself.

So the place to begin was in the intelligence sections. Smiling, Danforth stood up and strolled out into the hallway. Again he walked along, reading the signs on the doors. That didn't help much. The intelligence offices weren't labeled.

Danforth stood in the hallway and laughed. He had worked hard to figure out a course of action, and now he was going to fail because he couldn't think of a way to get to the intelligence officers. He needed a name.

And then insight hit for the second time. Morrow wouldn't tell him what Maxwell did, but that was obvious from where he had been only moments before they'd seen him. Maxwell was the name to use.

He walked back to the front of the building and found a general purpose office. Entering, he looked at the three clerks working there. "I need to find Maxwell."

"Who?"

"Maxwell. Intelligence."

The clerk glanced at the other two. "Either of you know a Maxwell?"

"Downstairs."

Danforth smiled. "Thanks." He left, walked down the hallway and then down the stairs, where he spotted an iron gate manned by an MP. Figuring there was nothing to lose, Danforth walked up and said, "I'm here to see Maxwell."

The MP shook his head. "Mr. Maxwell is out of the office now."

Danforth rubbed his face, then asked, "Anyone else I might see?"

"About?"

"An intelligence matter."

The MP consulted a list. "I think maybe you'd better check with Major Marsel up in room 109."

"Marsel?"

"Check with him," said the MP.

Danforth retreated, climbed the stairs, then walked down the hall until he found room 109. He stopped outside the closed door, but there was no sign on it. Reaching down, he touched the knob, then twisted it. Surprised when it turned, he opened the door and stepped in.

There was a rug on the floor, a couple of bookcases to one side, filing cabinets, two chairs in front of the desk and a half-dozen framed prints of the Army at war on the walls. A sergeant sat behind the desk. "Can I help you?"

Danforth moved into the office and nodded. "I was told to see Major Marsel."

"And you are . . . ?"

"Jason Danforth. I'm assigned to the news bureau here in Saigon."

The sergeant stood up slowly. Danforth noticed that his fatigues looked new and that he walked with a limp. He didn't look as if he'd been out in the sun recently. His skin was pasty white and he didn't look healthy. The sergeant opened a door behind the desk and leaned in.

A moment later he turned and said, "The major will see you. He said he'd give you five minutes."

"Plenty of time."

Danforth moved to the door and entered. This office was larger, darker and had a number of filing cabinets with combination locks. Marsel sat behind a gray desk that held a pen and pencil set, an in/out basket and nothing else.

Marsel was a skinny man, deeply tanned with blue eyes, sandy hair and fine features. He wore jungle fatigues that were slightly sweat-stained and wrinkled. "You are?" he asked.

"Jason Danforth. I've got a few questions I wanted to ask you, a few things to clear up."

Marsel pointed to one of the chairs in front of his desk. "Please be seated."

Danforth sat down and pulled a notebook out of his pocket. He flipped through it as if looking for something, then stopped, scrutinized the page and said, "I've been talking with Maxwell downstairs and wanted to get your opinion on a few matters before I went back to the office to write my story."

Marsel nodded, leaned back in his chair and steepled his fingers under his chin. "I'm not sure what help I can be. I find it strange that Maxwell would send you up to me. Very strange, indeed."

"Why's that?"

"I'm Army Intelligence and Maxwell's CIA. We rarely have that much in common. Oh, I'm copied on some of the classified documents that relate directly to my work here for the Army, but I don't report to him and he doesn't normally include me in his briefings."

"Would that include Phoenix?"

"That would include everything, though part of Phoenix is run through this office."

"So the Army has a hand in it?"

Marsel wheeled around in his chair so that he was facing the wall. He stared up at it as if there were something important written there.

"Of course the Army has a hand in it," said Marsel. "Actual implementation of the plan is through Special Forces and MACV-SOG."

Danforth tried to remember what he had been told the night before when he'd met Gerber and Fetterman. Morrow might have mentioned them in connection with SOG. He couldn't remember. He only knew they were Green Berets. "Would that include Captain Gerber?"

Marsel laughed. "I can't believe the amount of information Maxwell is handing out. I guess he's got a reason for it. Most of this stuff, you realize, is classified. Hell, we shouldn't even mention Phoenix in here."

"Because of the classified nature of the project."

"Exactly," said Marsel. "Wouldn't do to have the Vietnamese realize what we're doing, although any harm done to the Vietcong infrastructure can only be seen in a positive light by everyone in Saigon."

"Is Gerber involved in Phoenix?"

Marsel shrugged. "Indirectly. I doubt he knows what he's doing. He's got his orders, though no one has bothered to give him the grand scheme."

"Where's Gerber now?"

"Ho, you don't want much, do you? Where do you think he is?"

"Last night he was eating dinner at the Carasel Hotel, but I haven't seen him today."

"And you won't," Marsel said.

Danforth realized he wasn't going to get much farther. He'd need some specific information to keep Marsel talking, but he didn't have any. "What's Gerber's assignment?"

"Nope. I'm not going to give you that. I've probably said more than I should already."

"So where do I go to learn what Gerber is doing?"

"Downstairs to Maxwell. He should know. But I doubt he'll talk."

"Then you don't know," said Danforth.

Marsel turned again and looked at Danforth across his desk. "That won't work with me. I won't be humiliated into giving you answers. I may or may not know." he grinned. "Probably don't know."

Danforth flipped his notebook shut. "Then I'll have to go see Maxwell."

"That seems to be the only thing left for you to do."

Danforth stood up. "Thanks for your time." He wanted to grin because he had learned so much, but didn't. Instead, he moved to the door and opened it. Slowly he walked out, wanting to run, wanting to hurry down the hall to make more notes on what they had talked about, but he didn't want to tip his hand. He walked slowly, thinking that all those days in journalism school, drinking with the old hands who were brought in for guest lectures, had finally paid off. They had been right about how to get information. More than right.

FETTERMAN WAS ON THE POINT. He had slipped away from the main body and was moving through the jungle easily. He kept his head moving right and left, searching for signs that the enemy was around. Occasionally he looked up in the trees, making sure he wasn't walking under a sniper. Too many men had died because they didn't search the entire environment.

He stopped once, slipped to one knee and checked his compass, sighting on the light gray trunk of a distant tree. Putting the compass away, he began to move again, one foot in front of the other, stepping carefully, watching the rotting vegetation of the jungle floor, searching for booby traps out of habit. Charlie and the NVA wouldn't booby-trap the jungle in Cambodia because the Americans weren't authorized to operate there. But Fetterman wasn't taking any chances. He would continue to search.

The pace was steady, each man watching the back of the man in front of him, with the exception of Kepler, who was keeping his attention on the path they had followed. He made sure no one sneaked up behind them.

For ten minutes they worked their way through the jungle, moving as quietly as possible. Fetterman then held up a hand and the men scattered, forming a rough defensive ring while the master sergeant surveyed the jungle in front of them.

There was nothing unusual. Shafts of light filtered down, illuminating patches of jungle, turning them emerald-green. There were no signs of any other men. There were no indications that others were slipping up on them, no noises that Fetterman couldn't identify.

Satisfied that they were alone in that part of the jungle, Fetterman got to his feet and signaled the others. Cautiously they began to move again, everyone automatically searching the jungle for booby traps and ambushes.

They continued on for an hour, moving, stopping, moving again. The pace was slow because they were in Cambodia and the slightest mistake could kill them all. They avoided clearings and crossed a single path, which they ran across one at a time.

Fetterman stayed in the lead, halting only long enough to take compass readings or to listen for sounds of the enemy. They were lucky in one respect: they were in triple-canopy jungle where little sunlight penetrated to the floor. The thick tangle of undergrowth that choked some portions of the jungle hadn't grown here. A few bushes and ferns were in evidence, but much of the jungle floor was like parkland—easy to navigate while providing good cover.

The only real problems were the heat and humidity. The sunlight radiated through the canopy slowly and the dampness, without an easy avenue of escape, stayed close to the ground. The air nearly suffocated them. It sapped the strength of the men and made them light-headed. They sweated heavily, dehydrating rapidly in the oppressive jungle. They needed to drink water frequently to replenish their body fluids.

When they reached the first stream, Fetterman halted them again. He slipped down the bank and waded through the tepid water, feeling it fill his boots and soak the legs of his jungle fatigues. Fetterman didn't stop, but moved through the water, trying not to stir the silt at the bottom. A cloud of suspended mud drifting downstream could alert enemy soldiers.

On the other side he halted near the smooth trunk of a teak tree. Leaning his shoulder against the tree, he used his compass, then his map. The enemy camp wasn't that far away. If he increased the pace, they could reach it before sunset. A quick look at the camp in the light and then all night to get into position.

The others crossed the stream and joined him. Most of the men took off their boonie hats and dipped them in the stream. They poured water over their heads, soaking their hair and their jungle fatigues. Gerber knew that while this brief respite cooled them down and gave them new life, he had to make sure they didn't get carried away. Nothing was going to distract them from the mission.

On a signal from Gerber, Fetterman started out again. He stepped over the gnarled roots of a teak tree that stuck up through the rotting vegetation like the arthritic fingers of a giant. Avoiding a rocky outcropping, he slipped along its base, then began climbing up the gentle slope, trying not to scuff his feet and disturb the decaying vegetation on the jungle floor.

When Fetterman reached the top of the ridge, he halted. He waved at the men following him and they again scattered. Gerber moved forward carefully, crouching so that he was nearly bent double.

Fetterman knelt next to the trunk of a tree, staring down into the jungle. As Gerber reached him, he stretched out and crawled slowly to the top of the ridge. "What we got?" he whispered.

"I think we've arrived," Fetterman said, "providing Maxwell's information was correct."

Gerber slipped the binoculars from his case and surveyed the village spread out below them more than a klick away. Not much of a camp. There were a few rough hootches with thatched roofs. A couple of them stood on poles, notched logs for steps leading inside. There was a long building that might have been a barracks, another structure that looked like a radio shack, judging by the antenna wires, and a third building that was probably the cook house. Only a few men were visible.

Gerber examined the rest of the jungle around the camp. With the exception of the ridge they were on, the terrain seemed relatively flat. A shallow, narrow valley to the north was choked with brush and trees. Far to the west there was open ground with a hint of swamp.

"We'll have to get a little closer," Gerber said. "A couple of hundred meters."

Fetterman nodded to his left. "Looks like a good spot about three hundred meters away."

Gerber examined it with the binoculars. "Nope. Too easy to get at it from the camp." He continued his survey, then spotted a slight plateau about halfway down the slope where it dropped off rapidly. "There."

Fetterman followed his gaze. "Looks good. Easy escape for us with some good cover. Attack route up to us is tough, too. They'll have to go out of their way to get at us."

"Appears to have a good field of vision and it'll give us maybe a half klick, maybe a little more of a head start, after we make the shot."

"Yes, sir," said Fetterman, "providing you need more than one shot to take out the target."

"You could do better?"

"Merely commenting on the situation."

Gerber rolled and looked over his left shoulder. "Put Kepler and the security squad on top of the ridge behind us. That should put us in good shape."

"Slip into position tonight?" asked Fetterman.

Gerber still held binoculars to his eyes. "Yes. Get Kepler and his boys placed, then you and I can work down to the blind. Take all night to do it."

Fetterman watched the camp for a few minutes, then said, "Doesn't seem to be much activity down there. It's not a very big camp."

"I see two, three men," said Gerber. "One weapon."

"Maxwell might have gotten the location wrong."

"There's a camp here, just as Maxwell said. I imagine it's the right one."

"Doesn't seem possible that a man of importance would rise out of here."

"You can never tell," whispered Gerber. He put his binoculars away. "Let's get back to the others and get all this arranged."

"And eat," said Fetterman. "Tomorrow there won't be time to eat."

Gerber agreed. He slipped to the rear until the ridgeline blocked his view of the camp and then stood up. With Fetterman following, they hurried back to Kepler and the others. They had a lot of work to do before nightfall.

12

INSIDE THE CAMP NEAR
PHUM CHRES

The general sat with his back to a window that looked out into the darkening jungle. He was eating his dinner of roast monkey served on a large, flat palm leaf, using his fingers and wiping the grease on the front of his uniform. Occasionally he took a swig of wine from a clay goblet. His weapon, the pistol given to him by the North Vietnamese, was lying on the table near his left hand.

Swallowing a large bite, he said, "I don't understand the pressing need for night maneuvers."

"More training for the men," the NCO said. He was standing at parade rest in front of the general. "Teach them to survive in the jungle while searching for the Americans."

"They know how to do that," said Samphan.

"True, my General, but practice never hurts. Tomorrow, as they come in, you can address them and tell them of your pleasure in their training."

Samphan picked up the monkey, bit down and pulled off a mouthful of meat. "If you feel the need to take the men out for training, and if you're going to stay out with them, then do it. But I want everyone back here by noon."

"Certainly, General."

Putting the meat down, he wiped his hands again, smearing more grease on his shirt. He leaned back in his chair. "Just what is your plan?"

"A simple exercise. The men who were sent out today will be the pursued and the men going out tonight the pursuers."

"Noon tomorrow," said Samphan.

"Of course, my General." The NCO stood up and walked to the door. He hesitated there and glanced up at the ridgeline. There was no movement, but that meant nothing. The assassins would be there shortly, if they hadn't arrived already. All he had to do was wait patiently, his men in position to cut them off.

He walked over to the last hut, where seven men sat waiting. He crawled up into the hut with them and waited for the last of the light to fade.

MORROW STOOD just behind Danforth, watching as the man typed the last lines of his story. He pulled the page out of the typewriter and handed it to her. "Might as well get it all at once."

She scanned it quickly. "You can't print this."

"Why not? It's all true."

Morrow shook her head. "You can't say that. You've taken an overheard word and turned it into some kind of secret intelligence mission, which you don't describe, pinning the burden on Gerber and Fetterman and having it all controlled by Jerry Maxwell in his secret CIA headquarters buried in the bowels of MACV."

"That's exactly right."

"It's obviously not much of a secret if you found out about it so quickly."

Danforth held out his hand. "How about just giving me my story and I'll let the editor decide whether we run it or not. It's not your job to decide."

Morrow moved back and leaned against the desk behind her. She clutched the story in her left hand. "We have a policy about not writing about current operations. If, as you say, Gerber and Fetterman are in the field, then Hodges will spike the story until they return."

"Then I'll just take it elsewhere. Send it home and let them publish it." He reached up for the page again, but Morrow wouldn't let him have it.

"Being a journalist means we have a certain responsibility to uphold."

"Being a journalist," Danforth snapped back, "means protecting the people's right to know. You seem to have forgotten that."

"No," said Morrow, feeling her anger rise, "I haven't forgotten that. What's happened is that I've talked to people here, the soldiers fighting the war, and realized something. They're not the villains in this. You might think our involvement in Vietnam is wrong, or you believe it's right, but it doesn't matter. You ask the soldiers and you'll get a wide range of opinions, but most of them will tell you they're here in Vietnam because the government, the duly elected government of the United States, sent them."

"What's that got to do with my story?" asked Danforth.

"We rush to print this with Gerber and Fetterman in the field and we tell the enemy they're out there. Set them up as targets."

"There's nothing in my story that points to them."

"Oh, no?" said Morrow, flipping through it. "You suggest they might be in Cambodia. That marks them."

"Cambodia's a big country."

"Word games," said Morrow.

"Okay," said Danforth, holding up his hands as if to surrender. "What do I have to do to get my story back?"

"Let's check some of it out," said Morrow. "You've actually done a hell of a job putting together some facts, but we need to check them out."

"Maxwell wasn't around."

"Look," said Morrow, "this isn't a perishable story. No one else is on it. We don't have to rush into print without doing our homework. We get the facts wrong, and they're going to nail us to the wall, kill all our credibility. We have part of it right, it won't matter. We'll be dead on the lawn."

Danforth glanced down at the floor and then back up at Morrow. "We go over there together?"

"Absolutely."

"And you'll help sell the story to Hodges?"

"If we learn you're right on this, I'll help sell it to Hodges, on the condition we sit on it until I can talk to Gerber or Fetterman."

"What's our first move?"

Morrow handed the story back to Danforth. "I think we need to head back over to MACV and talk to Maxwell. He's the one who'll have the answers for us."

"I couldn't get down to see Maxwell."

Morrow grinned broadly. "I can."

THE RIDE BACK from Cambodia was uneventful, almost anticlimactic. They low-leveled to the border, and then a few klicks from it, popped back up to five thousand feet. Once clear, Maxwell relaxed, and forty minutes later they landed at the Air America pad.

He checked in, turned in the CAR-15 he'd carried and changed into his uniform of white suit, white shirt and narrow black tie. Without a word to anyone, he returned to his jeep and drove back to his office at MACV Headquarters.

Sitting in his office, he found it hard to believe that an hour earlier he'd been in Cambodia, meeting with a man who could have killed him, plotting a strategy that would end with several others dead. That was the thing about the Vietnam war. One minute you could be in danger, and the next sitting in an air-conditioned office working or in a club swilling beer and watching naked women dance.

At that moment, Maxwell realized what he had done. Up to that point, it had been an abstraction. He ordered men into the field and was then ordered to provide the enemy with information about those men that would neutralize them. He was ordering one group he worked with to kill another group.

But it went beyond that. He was giving information to Cambodians so that they could kill Americans. And not any Americans, but men he listed among his friends.

"Oh, God," he said. "What have I done?" He felt sick to his stomach and light-headed. He couldn't get enough air, and his face felt cold. The lights blurred. "Oh, God."

He stood up quickly and walked to the filing cabinets, not because he wanted something in them, but because he had to move. He pulled on a drawer and glanced at the bulging contents. Folders stuffed in every which way. He slammed it closed, whirled and then grabbed one of the Coke cans.

Without thinking, he lifted it to his lips, but there was nothing in it. He tried to crush it, failed, then threw it across the room. It struck the glass on his framed print, shattering it.

"Shit!"

The solution was to do something about it, let Gerber and Fetterman know they had been compromised without letting anyone else know he was blowing the whistle. He knew they would make contact with net control, if possible, in case there were sudden changes in the instructions. Information could be relayed to them through net control. The problem was that CIA operators monitored the frequency, too. Anything he sent out would be intercepted and would eventually come back to haunt him. His career would suddenly be over.

He dropped into his visitor's chair, bounced slightly, then settled down. He propped his head with his hand and felt sick. He was trapped. There was nothing he could do to help Gerber and Fetterman now. They were in the field and he was in Saigon.

He rubbed his face, pulling at his lips, trying to figure out a way around the problem. He needed to get Gerber and Fetterman out of the field now.

The knock at the door startled him. He leaped to his feet, his heart hammering. He felt like a thief caught inside the vault as the guards arrived. Rubbing his hands through his hair, he tried to straighten it, then adjusted his tie and the collar of his shirt.

He stepped to the door and opened it. He was about to speak when he saw that it was Morrow and felt the blood drain from his face. His breathing was rapid and shallow, and he thought he was going to be sick.

"Jerry," she said, moving toward him, "are you okay?" She remembered how he had looked when she had seen him at the embassy earlier that morning. "Are you ill?"

Maxwell whirled and moved toward his chair. He sat down and then bent at the waist, his head between his knees. He didn't speak to her.

Morrow moved forward and knelt beside him. She placed her fingers on his neck and started massaging. "Jerry?"

Maxwell held up his hand, then suddenly sat up. He leaned back against his chair, drawing in deep gulps of air. Sweat was beaded on his forehead and his face was chalk-white. "I'll be fine."

"What's going on?" asked Danforth from the door.

"Something I ate," Maxwell said.

"No," said Morrow. "You wouldn't still be this sick. It either passes, or you get sicker and then have to go to the hospital."

Maxwell pulled his handkerchief from his pocket and mopped his face. His breathing was more regular now. "I'm okay. Really, I'm fine now."

"You sure?"

Maxwell nodded and stood up. He moved to the chair behind his desk so that Morrow could sit in the visitor's chair. Leaning on his desk, he smiled thinly. "Sorry about all this."

"What's going on?" asked Morrow.

"Nothing. I'm just a little sick to my stomach." He hesitated, then added, "I had to take a quick flight this afternoon. Low level. I don't like that."

Morrow glanced at Danforth and then back at Maxwell. "Maybe this isn't the right time to push this."

"Or maybe it's the best time," said Danforth.

Morrow shot him a glance, then hesitated. "Anyway, Jerry, young Danforth has got his fingers on a story and we wanted to talk to you about it before we went to press."

"Oh, Christ, this is all I need."

"Then you know about the story," said Danforth. It wasn't a question.

"No, but if you're over here this late in the day, it can only be bad news."

"Go ahead, Jason," said Morrow.

"We're looking into Phoenix."

Maxwell felt his stomach flip again, but tried to keep his face blank.

"You mentioned it this morning. It's the code name for something directed against the infrastructure of the Vietcong and the NVA."

"How do you know that?"

"Major Marsel mentioned that," said Danforth.

"I'm afraid Major Marsel is misinformed. Phoenix," said Maxwell, talking rapidly, "is nothing more than a reconstruction of villages destroyed in the Tet fighting." He shrugged. "I suppose that could be considered as something directed against the Vietcong."

"That doesn't sound like something that would be a secret mission," Danforth said.

Maxwell shrugged again. "Can we go off the record?"

"I'd prefer to stay on the record," said Danforth.

"Then I have nothing more to tell you."

"Off the record," said Morrow.

"The reason we're keeping this under wraps is that we don't want the VC or NVA to know which villages we're going to move into. We want to get the repairs started, get the local men armed and trained, get the Army in there before the VC know we're moving. That's why things are hushhush now."

"Back on the record," said Danforth, "Marsel suggested that Gerber and Fetterman were involved in this. I don't see Special Forces officers going out to build villages."

Maxwell, whose color had improved slightly, asked Morrow, "You want to field that one, or shall I?"

"Special Forces troops are often involved in civic action projects, just as you were told last night."

"And," added Maxwell, "we want to recon the area before we move in with a large number of troops who aren't trained as combat soldiers."

"Marsel is in Army Intelligence, which suggests that Phoenix is an intelligence matter," said Danforth.

"The recon, of course, comes under the heading of an intelligence function. You have to remember that intelligence is more than spying. It's the gathering of all sorts of data and the dissemination of that data. All kinds, from the water temperatures of the South China Sea to the climatic changes we can expect as the seasons change."

"You have all the answers," said Danforth.

Maxwell rubbed at his face. "I'm supposed to have the answers. Sometimes I have to lie. Sometimes I have to do things I don't want to do, but Phoenix isn't one of them. You've got the story now, though I'd prefer that you hold it until we get our teams in place."

"That won't be a problem," said Morrow. She glanced at Danforth. "You satisfied?"

"No." He pulled his notebook from his pocket and flipped through it.

"Listen," said Maxwell, "this is too easy. Think about it. You blow in here with very little knowledge, and in a couple of hours you're able to put together this fantastic story about Phoenix, all based on overhearing one word. Correct?"

Danforth shrugged.

"Now, if it was something more nefarious, don't you think it would be harder to get information on it? You told me that Marsel just opened right up to you."

"He thought I already had the information."

"Doesn't matter. We don't go around discussing classified material with people we don't know, no matter what they seem to know. And that's without fail. Unless, of course, it's not a real security matter."

Morrow stood up then. "Are you satisfied, Jason?"

"I want to talk to Gerber and Fetterman when they get back," he said.

"They won't tell you a thing," said Morrow. "Not after the way you acted last night."

"I still want to see them."

"Good luck," said Morrow. To Maxwell she said, "We'll be going now. Will you be okay?"

Maxwell nodded. "I'll be fine. I'm going home in a few minutes. All I need is a good night's sleep."

Morrow moved to the door, then reached back and grabbed Danforth's sleeve. "Come on, we're going." As she stepped into the hallway, she turned. "I'll see you tomorrow, Jerry."

"Tomorrow. And please close the door."

Morrow did as he asked, leaving Maxwell alone in his office. For a moment he thought about what Danforth had said. It was obvious Marsel was talking out of turn. But that was something he could take care of with a couple of carefully chosen words. He couldn't get rid of him because that would make Danforth suspicious, but then Marsel was due to rotate out soon. Maxwell wouldn't tell him anything, and in a month or two Marsel would be on his way home.

That left only one other problem. How was he going to find Gerber and Fetterman and tell them to watch out for the ambush? How was he going to let them know their mission was common knowledge without letting Margarite and the others know it was he who'd told Gerber and Fetterman about it?

13

JUNGLES OF CAMBODIA
NEAR PHUM CHRES

They used the last of the daylight to slip into position, Kepler and the security team first, and then Gerber and Fetterman. Kepler and his men were scattered on the side of the ridge, near the top, so that they could keep an eye on the camp. They were clustered in pairs so that they covered two separate approaches, and were linked by the AN/PRR-9s and the AN/PRT-4s, the intrasquad radios. No one was to break radio silence, except in an emergency.

Once they finished with Kepler and his men, Gerber and Fetterman climbed back to the top of the ridge and watched the camp. Gerber again used the binoculars, scanning the camp and trying to memorize the locations of the hootches, radio shack and cook house. He searched for signs of guards, patrols or off-duty soldiers, but there were none. Smoke came from the cook house, and they had seen a lone man with no weapon walking around below them earlier, but it seemed the camp was deserted. Or nearly so.

Fetterman leaned close. "That radio shack bothers me."

"Me, too, but there's nothing we can do about it," answered Gerber.

Fetterman nodded, but Gerber knew what the master sergeant was thinking. A surreptitious raid down into the camp, a couple of well-thought-out cuts in cables, and the radio would be useless. The question was, did the benefits of wrecking the radio outweigh the unnecessary dangers of taking it out? Even a broadcast the instant the shot was fired wouldn't create much of a problem. The location of the sniper team and its security squad wouldn't be pinpointed.

"South Vietnam's what, eight, nine klicks away?" Gerber asked. "We can get there before they organize a proper search."

"Radio lets them alert everyone. They can get people behind us."

Gerber nodded. "Maxwell said we could get choppers in here. The Army sometimes crosses the border to assist units on this side, even without permission. Especially when they're in trouble and about to be eliminated."

"Radios are always a problem," said Fetterman stubbornly.

And Gerber had to agree with that, but he couldn't see tipping their hand by trying to infiltrate the camp. He just shook his head.

"Three hours," said Fetterman. "No roving guards, no patrols. I should be able to do it."

Gerber considered it, then shook his head again. "We're here as a sniper team. What you want to do violates the rules of the mission. We slip in, shoot and slip away."

"Yes, sir."

Fetterman moved to the rear, putting the ridgeline between him and the enemy camp. With Gerber covering him from that direction and the security squad protecting him from the other, he felt safe. As safe as any soldier that close to the enemy's base.

Fumbling with a P-38, Fetterman opened a can of boned chicken. He used the white plastic spoon that was packed with the meal and ate quickly, washing the meal down with water from his canteen. After he ate the white bread with jelly on it as dessert, he destroyed the cans and buried them and the remains of the meal. Finished, he crawled back to the top of the ridge.

Gerber glanced at him. "Let's move down now."

Fetterman nodded. "Go."

Gerber began crawling slowly over the top of the ridge, and then down toward the spot he wanted to use as the blind. The sunlight was fading rapidly, and the jungle was turning from a dim green glowing nightmare to a charcoal horror. The little breeze that had been rattling the trees died, and the birds, monkeys, insects and lizards slowed down. From the camp came the quiet hum of a generator, which didn't surprise either Gerber or Fetterman. If they had radios, they had to have a power source, and batteries weren't the best answer due to the environment.

Slowly they began to work their way down the hillside. Now it was important to make no noise. They had to slip through the jungle without disturbing it. In the morning, with the sun shining, anything they did to disturb the jungle would be spotted by an alert soldier in the camp below them. They had to be perfectly hidden.

After thirty minutes Gerber stopped. He lay quietly, the moisture of the decaying vegetation soaking through his jungle fatigues. Breathing slowly through his nose, he could smell the odors of the jungle. The undercurrent of death. The rotting of the vegetation that had fallen to the ground over the past few months and years. Soil in the jungle was notoriously poor, no more than an inch or two thick. It was the constant recycling of nutrients through the decay of dead plants and animals that supported the lush growth around them. That and rain, which was measured in feet per month rather than in inches per year.

The jungle was alive. Each acre held more types of plants, animals and insects than a square mile of land in the temperate zones, or in dozens of square miles in the desert. It seemed that danger was all around him, from the poisonous snakes to the poisonous insects, to the carnivores that would kill and eat anything.

And all that was complicated by the enemy soldiers, men living in the jungle whose lives revolved around the opportunity to find and kill Americans. One mistake, one slip, and they would be there, weapons blazing.

All that and more. Misdirected artillery. Falling bombs that were off course. Stray rounds fired from miles away. Gerber knew of one instance where a .50-caliber round had penetrated the corrugated tin of a hootch, bounced off the plywood wall and fell to the floor. It had to have been fired from four or five miles away. No one knew where it had come from.

Lying there in the middle of the Cambodian jungle, Gerber knew his life hung by a slender thread, but then that was his job. Go out into hostile territory, seek out the enemy, kill him and return to camp for the next assignment. Do it quickly, quietly and efficiently.

He took a deep breath, then slowly began to move again. Lifting himself slightly, he slid forward, then rested his body on the ground and started the process again. One hand, one foot, move the body and then relax, listening to the jungle.

Fetterman was right behind him. Gerber knew the master sergeant was there, but couldn't see him now that the sunlight was gone. He couldn't hear him. The master sergeant was a disembodied presence, following him down the slope toward the blind. Invisible, but there.

About halfway down the slope a light went on in the camp, then a second, and the hum from the generator increased. Gerber froze immediately. He stared down into the camp. There was no additional activity. Just the lights, dim glowing things that were little more than points of light. With the thick jungle canopy, the lights would be invisible from the air and therefore didn't endanger the camp.

Satisfied the enemy wasn't onto them, that no search parties were out, Gerber continued his trek. Slowly he moved down the slope, listening to the sounds of the night, sweat trickling down his back and sides, making his skin itch.

Finally he reached the plateau that he had seen from the top of the ridge. He crawled along it carefully until he came to the edge where he could look down into the camp. When Fetterman joined him, they rested for a moment and surveyed the plateau.

It was a small weed-choked area with a single large fern on one side, screening it from the south. The front dropped away sharply and then tapered gently out toward the enemy camp. It seemed as if they were on a platform overlooking the camp.

A couple of small saplings had been knocked down and a few rocks scattered around. Gerber slipped off to the left, then stopped. Fetterman moved off to the right so that the two men were separated by two or three feet.

Gerber pulled the sniper rifle from his shoulder and set it near his hand. He then carefully arranged his equipment around him so that he knew where everything was. Finally, using the binoculars, he studied the camp. There was very little light coming from it and no activity. It seemed as if everyone had left for some reason.

"I don't like this," whispered Fetterman.

"We can always get out," said Gerber.

"No, sir. I don't think we should abandon this mission. I just wish something would happen down there."

Gerber nodded, knowing Fetterman would never see the motion in the dark. The captain settled in to wait for the sun and his target. He knew it would be a long wait, but then that was what he was paid for.

JERRY MAXWELL DECIDED he couldn't stand it. His career was important to him. He had given up everything else for his career. He'd never married because the CIA didn't like their field people to do so. His friends were almost non-existent, mostly other CIA people and a few men in the Special Forces. With all the secrecy demanded by his job, it was hard to make friends. So in the end all Maxwell had was his career.

And now he was sickened by it. He had been through it all before. He had sent men out to die before. He'd even sent Gerber and Fetterman out on near-suicide missions. They had been the cover for the real mission once, but had succeeded in keeping their cover intact and gotten out alive. Even that time they'd had a fair chance of survival.

But this was completely different. They were being sacrificed without a fair chance. They were being thrown to the wolves.

Suddenly Maxwell brightened. He had the answer. Any message traffic initiated by net control or by him would be monitored by the CIA. That was SOP. But knowing the Special Forces, there would be another way to contact Gerber and Fetterman, a secret way the CIA wouldn't be privy to. The Special Forces had worked with the government and the CIA long enough to know that some backstabbing would take place. The men wouldn't want to be left with their butts hanging out. All he had to do was pass the word to SOG and let them notify Gerber and Fetterman.

He plucked his jacket from the back of his chair, checked to make sure that no classified documents were left exposed, then headed for the door. As he hurried down the hall, he realized that no one would think twice about his going to the SOG building, especially with men in the field. His cover was almost perfect.

He signed out at the iron gate and hurried up the stairs. In the parking lot he climbed behind the wheel of his jeep, unlocked it and started the engine. There were only a few vehicles in the lot, which was brightly lit. Barely visible off to the side were MPs, guarding against the possibility of VC sapper attacks.

Maxwell stopped at the street, checked the traffic, then pulled out. Normally he liked a leisurely drive through Saigon, especially at night because there was no telling what he would see. More than once he'd spotted a horny GI and a willing Vietnamese woman partially hidden in the shadows. Tonight he didn't have the time.

He wove his way through the traffic. There were horns behind him and rock and roll blaring from bars. The streets, as always, were filled with people. The air was hot and oppressive, but that was to be expected.

At the gate to Tan Son Nhut he slowed. The guard came out, glanced at him, then waved him through before he had come to a stop. That didn't bother Maxwell.

He reached the SOG building and parked the jeep. As he approached the door, he glanced toward the Air America pad, but there was no activity there. Inside the SOG building he walked down the narrow hall to the radio room. It was a small area with racks of radios against the wall. Tiny red and green lights glowed. Amber from the vu meters gave the two men sitting in front of the radios an eerie, ghostly look.

The men didn't pay any attention to Maxwell. They kept their eyes focused on their radios and the logbooks in front of them. A voice from behind asked, "Can I help you?"

Maxwell turned and saw another sergeant. He was a big, burly man with straight black hair and piercing eyes. It seemed as if he were looking right through Maxwell.

"Need to make a radio call. In private."

"This ain't AT&T. You want to make a call, you get the operator."

"Sergeant?"

"Ward," said the big man.

"Sergeant Ward," said Maxwell, "I want to be candid with you. I have to make radio contact with a team in the field, but we can't use normal channels."

"This still ain't AT&T."

"I understand that." Maxwell glanced around, saw an open door and stepped toward it. He reached inside and turned on the lights. "Can we talk in here?"

Ward followed him to the door, but didn't enter the room. Instead, he leaned against the jamb, his arms folded across his massive chest. It was then that Maxwell got a good look at him. His head seemed blunted on top, almost like an artillery shell. He had no neck, a massive jaw and a nose that looked as if it had been broken more than once. "What do you want?"

"This is a delicate matter," said Maxwell. "I can't afford to let anyone know I'm here telling you what I'm about to tell you."

"I don't have time for games."

Maxwell nodded. "Okay, Sergeant." He rubbed his face. "Do you know Captain Gerber and Sergeant Fetterman?"

"I've seen them."

"They're in the field now and I need to alert them that their mission might have been compromised. The enemy might know they're out there, but I don't want anyone to know I alerted them.''

"Why?"

"Why what?"

"Why don't you want anyone to know you're the one alerting them?"

"Good question." Maxwell pulled his handkerchief from his pocket and wiped his face to buy a bit of time. As he stuffed it back into his pocket, he said, "I think we've got a mole operating and I don't want him to know we know. That's why I came here instead of going through net control or using our own radio room."

Ward stood there impassively for a few seconds, then nodded. "Let's see what we can do."

They moved across the hall, and Ward talked quietly to one of the men at the radios, leaning down to whisper into his ear. Finally he glanced at Maxwell and shook his head. Maxwell feared the worst.

Ward pulled him aside and explained the situation. "They made their routine check with us, and that's it. No way to raise them now. They're in position and ready."

"Shit. Recall them," he said.

Ward grinned. "Can't. Even if we had radio contact, we couldn't just recall them. No authorization."

"I'll get you authorization," said Maxwell.

"Even if General Westmoreland himself appeared in this building, I couldn't recall them. Radio contact must be initiated at their end. Because of the changing nature of their situation, the men in the field control the radio."

"But they've been compromised," said Maxwell.

"Sir," said Ward, "I'm sorry as hell about that, but there's nothing I can do about it."

"Send in another team. Now. Tonight."

"Even if there were the men to do that, I couldn't send them in. No authorization."

"I told you I'd get you whatever authorization you need."

"I'm sorry, but there's nothing I can do here now. Not without more information and authorization from Nha Trang. We have to coordinate this so that we don't inadvertently wreck other missions."

"How long?" asked Maxwell.

"Twenty-four hours."

"No. Has to be faster. Has to be in the next six to twelve hours."

"Then there's nothing I can do."

Maxwell took a deep breath. "I'm talking about fellow Green Berets."

"I understand that."

Maxwell realized there was nothing he could do now. If he tried to arrange an Air America flight out there, Margarite would find out. There would be no way to cover his tracks, and his career would be in the toilet. The Special Forces had to do it for him. Get Gerber and Fetterman out.

He stared at the big man. "When do they check in again?"

"Sometime tomorrow."

"Then relay to them that they've been compromised. Make sure they get that message."

"Yes, sir." Ward started to turn to walk back into the radio room, but stopped. "This is very important to you."

"Very."

"I'm sorry we can't be of more help. We'll do what we can, but I can't promise you anything."

Maxwell stood there, feeling as if his world were coming to an end. He nodded. "Thanks for trying."

It began to look as if he might be throwing away his career for no good reason. But maybe he deserved it because of the way he had betrayed his friends. He deserved everything that would happen to him.

14

MACV HEADQUARTERS
SAIGON

Because there weren't many people around, and because it was the night shift, Danforth thought he might find someone inexperienced enough to talk out of turn. And he had been right about that. There was a skeleton staff on duty— captains, lieutenants and sergeants, new guys who had been in-country for two or three months, and only a couple of majors and lieutenant colonels who had been around for more than six months.

Danforth drifted along the corridors, looking into empty offices. He turned the lights on in some, stepped in and then retreated as he found banks of filing cabinets holding personnel or financial records. Some offices were Spartan in comparison to those of the senior officers. Others were loaded with furniture of the finest quality, but there was nothing lying around for him to read. The important papers and documents were locked away in safes.

Walking down the hall, he wondered if he should do a story on the money spent to keep senior colonels and generals happy. They had air-conditioned trailers supplied with TVs and stereos, and probably more than one of them had a woman stashed away, too. Taxes were wasted so that officers wouldn't be uncomfortable while in Vietnam.

But that could wait until later. Until he found out just what in hell was going on. Maxwell's story had sounded good on the surface, but Danforth had been around long enough to know a cover story when he heard one. And in this case, being in Vietnam for almost two days was long enough. What he needed to do now was penetrate the cover story.

He peeked into an office and found three men playing cards. All of them wore jungle fatigues. Two were enlisted men and the third a lieutenant. Danforth entered and leaned against a wall. "Anything happening here?"

The lieutenant, a young man so new to Vietnam that his fatigues were bright green and his bars were pinned to the collar rather than sewn on, looked up from his hand. He was already trying to grow a mustache, but he was fighting a losing battle.

"Nothing," he said.

"Can I ask you guys some questions?"

"What are you doing? Writing a book or something?" asked the lieutenant.

"I work for a newspaper."

"Fuck, Lieutenant," said one of the enlisted men. "Don't talk to this guy. You'll just get into trouble."

"Why do you say that?" asked Danforth.

The sergeant tossed his cards facedown on the low table. He picked up his Coke and drank from it, all the while keeping his eyes on Danforth. Like the lieutenant, the sergeant was a young man, twenty or twenty-one years old. He leaned forward, elbows on his knees.

"Every time one of you gentlemen of the press talks to one of us, somehow the words get twisted around or the story does, or both, and we come off looking like a bunch of amoral, murderous jerks."

"I haven't done anything like that," said Danforth. "I just want to know about Phoenix."

"The capital of Arizona," said the sergeant automatically.

Danforth shook his head and moved into the office. There was a desk to one side, but the men were sitting around a square coffee table, cards and MPC scattered on the top. He focused his attention on that. "It's also a program being run here."

"Well, we don't know anything about it," said the lieutenant quickly.

"You'd have to," said Danforth.

"See, Lieutenant," said the sergeant. "These guys think they know everything."

"I know enough to stay out of the Army," snapped Danforth.

Now the sergeant laughed. "What'd you do? Bribe some rummy doctor so that he'd give you a note saying you weren't fit for Army duty? Or are you in some kind of essential trade? Like writing bad newspaper columns about a war you know nothing about?"

"I know more about it than you do," said Danforth. "And I don't have blood on my hands."

"What's that mean?" asked the sergeant.

Before Danforth could answer, the lieutenant was on his feet. "How do we know you don't have blood on your hands? Maybe some of those lying stories you write have led to the deaths of soldiers. Maybe, because your lies stir up the public, the President changes his mind about bombing Haiphong and more enemy supplies get into the South."

"You can't bomb ports with the ships of neutral nations in them."

"Fuck," said the lieutenant. "What fairyland did you grow up in? Ships from Communist countries aren't neutral. Besides, I'll bet money that if they knew we'd sink the fucking ships, they wouldn't be there for long."

"I'd expect that kind of an attitude from a bunch of teen-age warmongers."

"You see, Lieutenant? I told you what would happen. Now this asshole is going to head back and write a story about what warmongers we are, never realizing that if we had our way, we'd go home."

"Then why don't you?" asked Danforth.

"Why don't you?" demanded the sergeant. "We didn't ask to come here, but we're here, trying to do our job. What are you here for?"

"To tell the American people the kind of job you're doing for them," said Danforth.

"Then tell it right," said the lieutenant. "Stop making up shit."

"We don't. I don't make up the stories I write."

The lieutenant pointed at the door. "Why don't you just get the hell out of here." He stopped and looked at the two men with him. "Better yet, why don't we escort you from the building."

"You have no right."

"Oh, but we do," said the sergeant. "This is a military installation, not some corporation. You have no right in here. Let's go."

Danforth didn't move for a moment. But then all three of the men facing him were on their feet. "Names," he said. "I want all your names."

But the men didn't answer him. They advanced on him until he turned and stepped into the hallway. The soldiers didn't stop. They came after him, herding him down the corridor until he reached the T intersection that led outside. Danforth turned and hurried toward the double doors. He hesitated, but the soldiers were still following him. They didn't stop until he was outside, about twenty yards from the doors. Then they stood there in the hall watching him.

Danforth realized he wouldn't get back into the building until morning. He turned and walked toward the MP shack near the road where he could catch a taxi back downtown. Just before he walked down the steps to the road, he glanced back. The three soldiers were still standing there, watching him, making sure he left.

"Well, shit," he said. "I guess that's it for the night."

IN THE HOUR BEFORE DAWN, the situation in Cambodia seemed to change. It was a subtle change, nothing that could be pinpointed. Maybe it was a sudden stirring of the cloud of insects or an undercurrent of noise created by the lizards and small animals scurrying to get away from the larger animals that were now prowling in the jungle. Maybe it was the cries of the birds that no longer sounded like morning calls but had taken on an urgency that suggested something was wrong.

Gerber twisted and focused his attention on the camp below him. The two lights had been extinguished around midnight. After that there had been no activity below, no sign that anyone had been put out on guard at any point during the night.

Fetterman slipped closer to the captain and used the binoculars. He shook his head slowly and whispered, "There's something odd going on down there. Maybe we should just get out."

"Only a little while until dawn," said Gerber.

"You ever in your whole career see a military camp run the way that one is?"

"Nope," said Gerber.

"There's no indication that our target is down there," said Fetterman.

Gerber rolled to the right and glanced up the hill. The jungle was charcoal. The bushes, ferns and trees were just beginning to become recognizable as the sun came up. "Animals are spooked."

Fetterman touched his forehead with his sleeve, wiping away the sweat. "Something isn't right."

Gerber fell silent and turned his attention back to the camp. Slowly the ground began to brighten. He was looking for signs that anyone was still down there. He didn't think they'd slipped away in the night.

"Captain, let's scrub this one. Get out now while we still have the partial cover of darkness."

For a moment Gerber was quiet, mulling over Fetterman's words. Gerber always trusted the sergeant's instincts. Besides, Fetterman was the quintessential soldier. Still, something about the situation kept bothering Gerber. "Just a bit longer," he whispered to Fetterman.

Gerber used the binoculars again, trying to find the enemy officer. He studied what he thought was the headquarters building. There was no movement there. The man had either left or was still asleep.

Then the intrasquad radio came alive. "Six, this is Two. We've got movement out here."

Gerber lifted the small handset to his lips. "How many?"

"Four, five guys to the right and four or five guys directly in front."

"Military?"

"Armed. We've spotted a couple of weapons. They're fanning out about fifty, sixty meters away from us now."

"Roger." He glanced at Fetterman.

"That would explain it," said Fetterman. "Everyone's out of the camp and circling up behind us."

"But they don't seem to know we're here. We could take the shot."

"They're between us and the escape route."

Gerber again looked down into the camp. The charcoal was now a light gray. The buildings were obvious and some of the smaller details were taking shape. The first colors were beginning to show, and there were white wisps of fog, some clinging to the ground and some up in the trees.

Gerber frowned. "We cut the security loose and then shift around the ridge here. Then when we make the shot, we escape-and-evade first to the west and then south and finally to the east, heading for South Vietnam."

"That would fool them," said Fetterman.

"Six, we have more movement," said Kepler on the radio.

"Roger. Are they approaching?"

"Negative. I don't think they know we're here. They're moving carefully, but not toward us."

"Roger. Keep me posted."

Fetterman leaned close, his voice barely audible. "Movement below us."

Gerber twisted around and studied the camp. One man was walking out of a hootch toward the cook house. He stopped at the door and stood facing away from it, one hand to his crotch, the other pressing into the small of his back, taking his morning leak.

"More of them moving in, Six," said Kepler.

"Let's get out," Fetterman said.

There was movement then in the command hootch. Just a shape passing in front of the door. Gerber raised the Winchester, quickly snapped the covers off the scope and tried to find the target.

"Ah, Six," said Kepler, "we've got fifty men on the hill now. At least fifty."

"Sir," hissed Fetterman.

And then Gerber saw the target—a single man in a khaki uniform. There was no doubt that the man stepping down the notched log was the officer they were supposed to kill. He was moving slowly and was a perfect target.

But Gerber didn't bother to chamber a round. He watched as the man walked across the compound and then disappeared into the cook house.

"Six, this is Four."

"Go, Four," said Gerber, recognizing Tyson's voice.

The voice was barely audible. A quiet whisper. "We've got VC in front and behind us."

"Roger. Stay chilly."

Fetterman put his lips next to Gerber's ear. "We've been had."

Gerber glanced at the master sergeant, but understood exactly what he meant. It was no accident that the camp was vacant. Somehow the enemy knew they were coming and had taken steps to intercept them. The only thing he didn't understand was why they hadn't been jumped already.

"This is Four," whispered Tyson. "They're circling toward us, searching."

"Roger," said Gerber. "We're on our way."

Fetterman shifted and picked up his spare canteen and the three grenades he'd placed on the ground in front of him. "I'm set."

Gerber did the same, picking up the equipment he'd spread out. He carefully packed the Winchester in its case. The sniping weapon wouldn't be any good in a close-quarters fight in the jungle. The bolt-action nature of the Winchester gave the firepower edge to the enemy. He wanted to use the spare M-16. With the Winchester stored, he took the assault rifle from Fetterman. "Go," he told the master sergeant.

Fetterman eased back from the edge of the plateau, crawled to the slope and then slowly got to his feet. Gerber followed him and waited until the master sergeant started up the slope. When Fetterman was ten yards away, Gerber began to move again. He clutched his M-16 in both hands, his thumb near the selector switch. He had a round chambered and the selector on single-shot.

As they climbed to the top of the ridgeline, Gerber listened for the enemy. There was movement in the jungle, but it was caused by animals on the jungle floor and monkeys and birds in the canopy above them. Insects swarmed around them, darting in and out, tasting the salt of their sweat.

At the top of the ridgeline, Fetterman dropped to the ground. As Gerber neared, the master sergeant pointed at the center and then toward the right twice. Each time he was showing Gerber where enemy soldiers waited. They were all looking back down the slope as if they expected the Americans to come from that direction.

Fetterman touched the hilt of his knife, dragged a finger across his throat, then pointed at one of the enemy soldiers. Gerber thought about it. The rifle would take them out quicker, but it would announce his presence to the enemy. The best way was the knife, if they could maintain the stealth.

Gerber nodded. Fetterman grinned, then began moving to the left, where the lone soldier stood. Gerber took the handset of his AN/PRT-4 and whispered, "Four, take the two on the south side. Knives."

There was a double click in answer. It meant that Tyson had received the message and understood. Gerber slipped the radio into his pocket, then began to work his way down the slope. He moved quietly, keeping his eyes focused on a point to the right of the enemy. He could see the man, but wasn't staring at him. Gerber knew that an unwavering stare sometimes alerted a man to the presence of an enemy soldier.

He slipped through the undergrowth, avoiding the small plants that would rustle against his clothes, the small sticks lying on the jungle floor that could snap and the long, hanging vines that could tangle in his pack and equipment and stop him. He moved one hand and then one foot, crawling along, glancing directly at his adversary once, twice and then away again.

The enemy soldier shifted, turned and looked right at Gerber, but didn't see him. He glanced at the jungle, then up at the canopy, which glowed bright green under the morning sun. Then he settled back, watching the jungle in front of him.

Gerber inched forward until he was only a few feet from the enemy soldier. Carefully he drew his knife, slipping it from the scabbard taped to his harness. As the blade came free, Gerber came up onto the balls of his feet and reached out with his left hand. In a single, fluid motion he grabbed the enemy from the rear. His left hand covered the soldier's mouth and pressed against his nostrils. He dragged the Cambodian back onto the fulcrum of his knee, pressing it into the enemy's spine. The right hand flashed, slicing into the soft flesh of the throat with a quiet whisper that only Gerber could hear.

Blood spurted and covered his hand. The man sagged against Gerber's knee. He whipped his knife around and jammed it into the soldier's back. It slipped in over the right kidney, penetrated the lung and sliced into the heart. Gerber lowered him to the ground, then crouched next to the body, almost like a jungle cat over a kill. The captain stripped the man of weapons and equipment. He didn't want them, it was SOP to deny them to the enemy.

Fetterman loomed suddenly out of the jungle. One of his sleeves was covered with blood. Gerber raised an eyebrow in question, and Fetterman shook his head. It wasn't his blood.

Together they moved south. Both enemy soldiers there were dead, too. Surprise had been complete. For some reason the enemy didn't expect an attack from Gerber's men. Maybe they didn't know about the security guard. Maybe their information was incomplete.

Leaning close to Braver, who had appeared with Tyson, Gerber asked, "That it?"

The younger man nodded. "Clear now."

Gerber took his intrasquad handset out and turned it on. "Zulu Two, move south."

There was an instance of silence and then two quiet, acknowledging clicks.

Fetterman whispered, "What about the target?"

"Forget it. We're getting out now," Gerber told him.

Braver appeared and leaned close. "There's another two of them in front of us now."

"Take them," said Gerber.

Braver grinned evilly. He nodded and disappeared into the jungle.

Fetterman followed the younger sergeant. A moment later he reappeared, carrying another AK-47 and a pouch of spare magazines, which was covered with blood.

Gerber nodded at the master sergeant and used his radio again. "Two, say location."

"Fifty meters to your right. Coming in."

Gerber waited, then saw Kepler moving toward him. Braver was off to the east, coming at him. The team was together again. As everyone approached, Gerber pointed at Fetterman and then to the south. The master sergeant understood. He began moving in that direction to take the point.

Kepler halted and held up a hand, then pointed at Sergeant Thai, telling Gerber he'd form the rear guard with the Vietnamese NCO. Gerber nodded.

Quickly they strung out, working their way south away from the enemy camp and the force spread out on their line of retreat to Vietnam.

Gerber began to relax. They had lucked out and were now clear. Suddenly Fetterman halted, then pointed at him. Gerber hurried to the front of the short column and knelt next to the master sergeant, who indicated the way ahead.

Below them, along the bank of a stream, Gerber saw a squad of enemy soldiers, each armed with an AK. He wasn't worried about that. He was sure they could take the enemy, especially with surprise on their side, but the firing would alert the others searching for them.

Kepler appeared then and leaned close. "I have my silenced pistol."

Gerber nodded. "I'll cover from here with the sniper rifle. You get into trouble and we'll support."

"Give me Thai. We'll cut a path for you."

"Go," said Gerber.

Kepler waved Thai forward, and the two of them began to descend toward the stream. Fetterman whispered, "You think he'll do it?"

"All we can do is wait," said Gerber. "Wait and hope our luck doesn't desert us."

15

THE JUNGLES INSIDE
CAMBODIA

Kepler and Thai crept down the hillside, moving slowly in the growing heat of the morning. Both were sweating heavily, but neither noticed it. Their attention was drawn to the enemy soldiers spread out in a loose string along the bank of a bubbling stream. The closer Kepler and Thai got, the more the noise from the stream covered any sound they might make. The choice of the ambush site wasn't a very good one.

Kepler pushed forward until he was nearly on the same level as the ambushers. Through gaps in the bright green vegetation he could see two of the enemy soldiers. One of them seemed nervous, moving, shifting and scratching. Each movement drew attention to him.

The other was quieter. He turned his head slowly once toward the nervous man, but said nothing. Carefully he changed position so that he was facing up the hill, his AK cradled in his hands.

Kepler braced himself against the trunk of a tree and raised his silenced pistol. He aimed at the temple of the man closest to him and squeezed the trigger. The weapon coughed and the man suddenly spasmed. He threw his rifle down and rolled over, blood fountaining from the hole in his head.

As the man fell, his partner turned. He swung his AK around as if afraid they were being attacked. Kepler aimed at his chest and fired again.

The impact hurled the man back violently. He looked down at the spreading crimson stain. Kepler put a second round into his face, then disappeared into the dense vegetation.

But the noise of the man falling in the jungle alerted his friends. One of them shouted, and there was a burst of fire from an AK. Kepler heard the bullets snap through the jungle over his head.

Thai opened fire then, using his M-16. Another Cambodian fell. As he dropped, he put a wild burst into the jungle floor in front of him.

From behind them came a single shot. Kepler knew it was Gerber, using the sniper rifle to take out enemy soldiers. Kepler stuffed the silenced pistol inside his jungle jacket, the hot barrel burning his bare skin. He raised his M-16 and pulled the trigger, firing into the muzzle-flashes in front of him.

The firing intensified. Thai pulled a grenade, yanked out the pin and threw the weapon toward the water. It landed on the bank and detonated. Dirt and water fountained. Shrapnel cut through the air. One man screamed and fell back into the water, blood spreading around his head almost like a halo.

Then suddenly the Cambodians were running. There was no command to retreat. One of the soldiers threw down his rifle and sprinted away, leaping first over the shallow stream. Close on his heels were two more followed by the rest of the men. The shooting tapered until it was only Thai's M-16 firing as he tried to drop some of the fleeing men.

"COMING UP BEHIND US, Captain," said Fetterman.

Gerber whirled and saw movement in the jungle behind him. There was a burst from his right, and then movement stopped immediately.

"Let's go, Fetterman, take us out."

"Yes, sir."

"Braver, go!" yelled Fetterman.

The young man ducked under a low-hanging branch, pushing the vines away with the back of his hand as he hurried down the slight slope. One hand waved in the air, as if he was riding a bronco and trying to keep his balance. He disappeared into the jungle. Tyson was right behind him.

"Captain?"

"Go!" said Gerber. "Go!" He glanced at Fetterman as the master sergeant followed the other two men. When Fetterman vanished into the jungle, Gerber turned and raised his rifle, watching the jungle around him.

There was movement, and Gerber fired a shot at it. It stopped abruptly, but Gerber didn't think he'd hit anyone. Then someone fired at him. Rounds slammed into a tree close to him. Gerber spotted the muzzle-flashes. Using the scope, he found the enemy soldier. A bit of his face showed through the dense bushes and ferns between them. Gerber pulled the trigger and heard the enemy soldier scream in sudden pain as his head exploded and then disappeared.

Gerber whirled and ran. He slipped down the slope, moving as fast as he could. Behind him the enemy had opened fire, ripping the jungle apart. Rounds from AKs snapped overhead, hit the trees and punched through the leaves. Bits of debris rained down.

At the stream Gerber caught up to Fetterman. He passed the master sergeant just as he opened fire on full-auto. Fetterman, using an AK, burned through a magazine, then yanked it from the weapon. He tossed that into the water and reloaded.

"A hundred yards!" yelled Gerber.

"Understood."

Gerber leaped into the water, then onto the other bank. He knelt and watched the hilltop on the other side. The enemy seemed to have halted their advance.

Fetterman caught up with him, and together they moved on, following the two younger men who, in turn, followed Kepler and Thai.

They ran on for a hundred meters and then dived for cover. Gerber looked through the sniper scope but couldn't see the enemy. Next to him Fetterman used the binoculars. Both men were breathing hard, partly from sprinting through the jungle and partly because of the humidity.

Seeing nothing, Gerber keyed the intrasquad radio. "Two, you see anything?"

"Negative. Clear to the front."

"East?" asked Gerber.

"Clear," said Kepler.

"Roger, wait there." He slapped Fetterman on the arm and hooked a thumb over his shoulder.

Fetterman nodded and got to his feet, running on toward the head of the column. When he got ten or twelve yards away, Gerber got up and started running, too.

In the lead, Kepler turned east. He slowed down to a fast walk, paused once, listened for signs of pursuit, then started off again.

Gerber let the men get a good lead on him, then dropped off. He listened to the jungle behind him. There was an occasional burst of fire—five or six rounds and then silence. Each time the birds screamed and monkeys shrieked, leaping from tree to tree as if to escape the rifle fire.

But it was all behind him half a klick or more. There was nothing to see up there. It looked as if the enemy had found a place they liked and weren't going to venture from it.

Gerber turned and followed the path blazed by Kepler and the others. They had slowed even more, now trying for stealth. Gerber saw a flash in front of him. But it was only Braver turning his face to the rear to make sure nothing had happened to the captain.

After thirty minutes they halted again, forming a loose circle. Gerber knelt near Fetterman, breathing heavily for several moments. He checked the map with sweat-damp hands and studied his compass. "An hour or less to South Vietnam."

"And then?"

"We catch a ride and head on to Saigon. I'll borrow the .22 from Kepler and we'll go talk to Maxwell."

"You think he's responsible?"

Gerber nodded. It was the only answer that explained the facts. There was no other way the enemy could have gotten in behind them like that, right on the line of retreat, without some prior knowledge. They had then stopped and waited for something, almost as if they wanted Gerber to fire the shot before attacking.

"Maxwell's had it," said Gerber.

MAXWELL SPENT THE NIGHT at the SOG building. At first he hung around the radio room, hoping Gerber or Fetterman would check in, but that didn't happen. Finally he gave up and walked to the dayroom, telling the men on radio watch to alert him if Gerber called.

Then he tried to get some sleep, but found it impossible. He lay down on the couch, looking up at the darkened ceiling. He wasn't really tired. His eyes burned from lack of sleep. And the noise from the airfield didn't bother him.

He'd slept through mortar attacks before because he'd sub-consciously realized they were moving away from him.

At a fire support base he'd once slept through an hour-long barrage. But here in the SOG building he couldn't sleep, even when the roar of the fighters faded. Instead, he lay there and watched the dancing lights from the airfield as they played across the ceiling. Red and blues and whites and greens. Navigation lights from aircraft wings and flashing lights from emergency vehicles, or just headlights.

The problem wasn't the noise. The problem was Gerber and Fetterman in the field with the Cambodians knowing where they were and with orders to find and kill them. That was the problem. So he spent the night on the couch, watching the lights and listening to the jets and the artillery and the cars and the jeeps.

Eventually he got up and opened the refrigerator. There were cans of beer and Coke, half a loaf of bread and a jar of mustard. Maxwell took out a beer, opened it and drank half of it in a single pull. It didn't help. At dawn he walked back to the radio room, but the sergeant sitting there shook his head.

"Anything at all?" asked Maxwell.

"Everything's quiet. If they're in position and there are no problems, there would be no reason to call."

"Damn," said Maxwell. "They've been compromised."

"Yes, sir." He glanced back at the radio. "If they check in, I can order them out. There's no reason for you to wait around here."

Maxwell looked at his watch and then ran a hand through his hair. It was greasy and wet. He took a deep breath. "I'll be over at MACV. If you hear anything, get in touch with me."

"Yes, sir. Happy to."

Maxwell stood there for a moment longer, looking at the radios and the needles bouncing on the vu meters. There was a burst of static and then silence.

Finally he turned and left. He walked down the hall to the door, then stepped into the muggy early-morning heat. He watched two Phantoms streak down the runway and leap into the sky, leaving twin trails of thick black smoke.

He didn't understand the depression that was weighing him down. Gerber and Fetterman would be able to get clear. They had been sent into situations that were more difficult and still managed to get themselves out. They were professional soldiers who knew how to survive.

He climbed into his jeep, unlocked it, then started the engine. For a moment he sat there, looking at the sticky film that had formed over everything during the night. He pulled out his handkerchief and wiped off his hands, then the steering wheel.

Until Gerber and Fetterman made a radio check there was nothing he could do. The message had been left. It would be relayed. All he could do was wait.

GERBER NODDED and Fetterman took the point. The men followed him with Gerber in the rear. During the fifteen minutes that they rested, there was no sound that suggested the enemy was close.

Their progress was slower now as they worked their way through the jungle, stopping frequently, listening for the enemy. But there seemed to be no pursuers. The periodic firing from behind had stopped. It was as if the Cambodians had vanished.

Fetterman halted as they came to the edge of the jungle. The men spread out naturally, and Gerber worked his way forward, dropping to the ground next to the master sergeant.

"I think we're back in South Vietnam," Fetterman said.

Gerber looked at his map, then nodded. "We need an LZ. We might as well secure this one."

"Be interesting to see if there are any aviation assets standing by to assist us."

"Certainly will." Gerber got to his feet and worked his way over to Kepler. "I want you and Thai to check out the LZ to the north."

"Yes, sir."

"Slow and easy. Right now we don't have any troubles."

"Yes, sir."

As Kepler and Thai moved off, Gerber found Braver and Tyson. He pointed at Braver. "You're with me. Tyson, you hold here with Fetterman, securing this location."

Tyson nodded.

Together they began to slip along the edge of the LZ. Unlike some landing zones in the Central Highlands, this one wasn't ringed by enemy bunkers. Charlie sometimes built defenses in the locations he knew Americans would use. In the Central Highlands there were a limited number of landing zones and the VC booby-trapped, mined and built bunkers around them. Here, farther south, there were dozens, hundreds of LZs, and the enemy didn't waste time with booby traps and bunkers that might never be used.

They slowly worked their way through the trees, around the bushes and dodged the wait-a-minute vines. Close to the edge of the jungle the vegetation was thicker than in the deeper, triple-canopy areas. It made the search hard work. The sun added to the discomfort, as did the humidity.

They stopped at the southern side, and Gerber crawled to the very edge of the LZ and looked down the long axis to the north. There were only a few trees in the center—saplings, a carpet of grass, two or three feet tall, nothing that would damage a helicopter.

They continued on then, finally meeting with Kepler on the far side. Kepler waved at Gerber and shook his head. He'd found nothing of interest on his trip around the northern side of the LZ.

Gerber nodded, then pointed at the far side where Fetterman and Tyson waited. "You first, then Thai, Braver and me."

"Yes, sir."

Kepler moved to the edge of the LZ, crouched in the bright sunlight and quickly checked all his equipment. Satisfied everything was fastened down, he got to his feet, ducked his head, almost as if nodding to the starter at a track event, and then leaped out into the thigh-high grass of the LZ. He began a slow jog, his head swiveling right and left, examining the deep grass and the ground under it, searching for signs of recent digging, for trip wires and pressure plates, or signs that someone had walked through the LZ recently. There was nothing.

Thai followed Kepler, taking a slightly different path, searching more of the landing zone. Braver did the same, and finally Gerber, bringing up the rear, completed the cycle. There was nothing on the landing zone to indicate anyone had ever walked on it.

When the team was gathered on the other side, they spread out in a circle for security. Gerber took out the URC-10, extended the antenna and pushed the button on the side. Holding it close to his lips, he said, "Crusader Ops, Crusader Ops, this is Zulu Six, over."

There was a moment of silence, then a tinny voice. "Zulu Six, this is Crusader Ops. Go."

"Zulu Six is ready for pickup."

"Roger, Zulu Six. Wait one."

Gerber pulled his map out and twisted it around. He was ready when Crusader Ops came back.

"Zulu Six, say location."

Gerber ran his finger down the map, figuring the coordinates and subtracted Jack Benny's age from all of them, then said, "Up from Benny's age. Two five one seven."

"Understand up from Benny's age. Wait one."

Fetterman grinned at him. "I don't know if we fool anyone with that simple code."

"How many VC are going to know Benny's 'age' is thirty-nine, or for that matter who Benny is?"

Fetterman shrugged.

"We're inbound your location in one five minutes. Will you throw smoke?" the voice on the radio crackled.

"Roger, smoke."

"Say condition of Lima Zulu."

"Lima Zulu is cold."

"Roger, cold."

Gerber waited for a last transmission to tell him that Crusader Ops was finished, but it didn't come. The aviation units treated the radio as if it were a telephone, never saying over or out when they were finished. They talked and then let go of the mike button. Gerber had once asked a pilot about the matter and he'd said that saying over and out and some of the other things did nothing except use up valuable airtime with no real purpose served. When a hundred men were all using the same frequency and the bullets were flying, no one really had time for all the bullshit radio procedures.

Now that the choppers were coming, Gerber relaxed slightly. He let half the men off security, meaning that only he, Fetterman and Kepler were keeping watch. It was enough.

"Zulu Six, this is Crusader Lead, we're zero three from your location. Can you throw smoke?"

"Roger, smoke."

As he finished, Fetterman slipped to the ground beside him. "We've got a problem. Someone's coming up from the south. At least a full squad."

"Shit. How far off?"

"No more than two hundred meters now. Maybe less."

Gerber keyed the mike. "Crusader Lead, be advised we have enemy movement to the south of the Lima Zulu."

"Are you in contact?"

"Negative."

"Roger. We're inbound."

Fetterman said, "They might be waiting for the choppers."

"No way we can get back to eliminate them now. Maybe we should try to have the guns hose down the jungle."

Before Fetterman could respond there was a single shot and then a long, ripping burst.

Gerber squeezed the URC-10, nearly crushing it. "Crusader Lead, the LZ is now hot." With that he jammed the radio into his pocket and pulled his M-16 closer. The sniper rifle was slung over his back.

"This way," said Fetterman. He was up and moving through the jungle.

Gerber followed him, keeping low. They dodged from tree to tree, using the available cover. Gerber saw movement through the trees and dropped to the ground. He listened as someone worked closer to him. He popped up, saw the enemy soldier and fired twice. Blood blossomed on the man's face and chest as the Cambodian fell into the bushes.

An RPD opened up then, a long, sustained burst. The bullets snapped overhead, shredding the bark from the trunks and tearing at the leaves. Bits of debris floated down.

"Over here," said Fetterman. He fired a short burst, then a longer one. There was a single piercing scream that ended abruptly. A body crashed to the ground.

Firing erupted throughout the jungle—AKs and RPDs with almost no answering fire from the M-16s. Gerber, still facedown on the jungle floor, grabbed at one of his grenades. He yanked the pin free, then lay there, holding the weapon and listening to the patterns of enemy firing. It sounded as if the RPD was to his left, close to the edge of the LZ where it would be in a position to either fire on the helicopters or on Gerber's men in the trees.

He drew his legs up so that his knees were nearly touching his chest. Then he popped up, glanced to the left and threw his grenade as hard as he could. As he released it, he dropped again, pressing himself to the jungle floor.

"Grenade!" he shouted, warning those on his team.

An instant later there was a explosion. Dirt mushroomed and then fell back, sounding like the beginning of a rainstorm or frying bacon.

The answer was a long burst from the RPD. A few rounds flashed over him harmlessly. There hadn't been much chance that he could destroy the gun by throwing his grenade without first having identified the machine gun nest.

A new sound joined the others—rotor blades. The helicopters were getting close. But they wouldn't land without someone throwing smoke. And they'd be able to hear the firing, even over the sound of the turbines and the beat of their rotor blades. It was surprising how much could be heard when life depended on it.

"Tony, let's pull back. To the north."

"On my way."

"Kepler?"

"Here."

"Follow Tony. We've got to open up the ground between us and the enemy."

"On my way."

Gerber slipped to the rear toward the thick trunk of a palm tree. He got to his feet and opened fire with his M-16, burning through one magazine, letting all twenty rounds go in short, quick bursts. Then he reloaded and did it again.

The enemy returned fire—a dozen AKs and the RPD, all directed at him. Gerber threw himself to the ground and rolled away. He heard the rounds slamming into the trees around him.

As he scrambled to the rear, he heard firing behind him. It would be Fetterman and the boys trying to take some of the heat off him. When he reached them, he stopped and pulled out the radio.

"Crusader Lead, we're under attack."

"Roger. Guns on the way. Can you throw smoke?"

"Roger, smoke."

"We're at the edge of the trees!" shouted Fetterman.

Gerber didn't respond. He began to crawl in that direction, stopping after ten or twelve meters. Firing was tapering again. The enemy was on the move.

"Use the CS," ordered Gerber.

"Wind direction?" Kepler asked.

Gerber shook his head. He had no idea of the wind direction. The breeze was too light to tell where it came from, especially under the trees. If it was from the wrong direction, the CS could be blown back in their faces.

"Kepler! Throw the smoke!"

There was movement to the left, and Kepler tossed a grenade into the open LZ.

Gerber was on his feet then, watching the enemy positions. He spotted one man and fired at him. The man dived for cover. Others opened up again, shooting at Gerber.

"Use the CS," called Kepler.

"Zulu Six, ID green."

"Roger, green."

"Inbound."

Gerber hesitated for a moment. The others, Fetterman, Braver and Tyson, threw CS grenades. There was a distant popping as each of the canisters exploded, pouring out the CS.

He was up and running then, dodging the trees and bushes, pressing toward the LZ. Firing was sporadic. Clouds of grey-white gas billowed, spreading southward where the enemy soldiers hid.

The choppers appeared over the south edge of the trees. They screamed along at full speed, then dropped closer to the ground, aiming at the smoke, engines roaring.

The lead helicopter seemed to roll over on its side and then slowed rapidly. It shuddered for a moment, then righted itself, settling to the ground. As the skids touched down, Kepler ran from the trees, head down, one hand holding onto his boonie hat. He carried his M-16 by the sight so that he looked like a commuter running for a morning train with the weirdest briefcase in the world.

Thai and Braver followed him. Gerber arrived at the edge of the jungle almost at the same time as Kepler reached the helicopter. He stepped up on the skid, then launched himself into the cargo compartment, rolling into the interior.

Fetterman was beside Gerber. "Looks like we're going to get out of this."

A sudden burst caught Braver in the back, lifted him and threw him to the ground. He seemed to bounce and then was still. Kepler leaped out of the helicopter and ran toward the downed man as Tyson grabbed him under the arm to drag him to safety. Thai whirled, leveled his rifle and opened fire, burning through his magazine on full-auto.

The door guns on the choppers began to fire. Tongues of flame three feet long stabbed out, barely visible in the bright sunlight. Ruby tracers flashed as the guns continued to hammer.

And green tracers answered. The RPD was shooting again. Rounds slammed into the tail boom of the lead chopper, punching through it easily. Gerber touched Fetterman on the shoulder and both of them whirled and sprinted into the LZ. Bullets snapped over their heads. They reached Thai, and the Vietnamese striker turned and ran with them. They caught up to Kepler and Tyson, who were dragging Braver. Bloodstains covered the back of his uniform.

"Go!" yelled Kepler.

Gerber raced past him and then spun. He dropped to one knee and stared at the jungle. There was movement behind the trees—men running to get into position, muzzle-flashes. Gerber opened up, firing in short bursts. He emptied one magazine, dropped it from his weapon, slapped another home, then opened fire again.

And then the gunships rolled in. One Huey came out of the sun and dived at the trees, rockets firing. The first two rockets dropped short of their target. Fountains of orange outlined in brown leaped into the air.

The next pair exploded in the trees. The jungle looked as if it had erupted as yet more rockets exploded. The noise of the detonations rocked the LZ. Machine guns chattered, tearing up the ground, and ruby tracers poured into the trees.

Kepler and Tyson reached the chopper and tossed Braver into the rear. As the body rolled in and Kepler leaped up, he shouted, "Let's go!"

Thai was right behind him, as was Fetterman. Gerber emptied his magazine into the trees and then whirled. He stepped onto the skids and the chopper lifted off. Fetterman grabbed Gerber's harness and hauled him up and in. Both sprawled on the floor of the cargo compartment. Gerber's face was only inches from Braver's. It was obvious that the young man was dead. His staring, unseeing eyes were glazed.

Behind them the LZ and surrounding jungle exploded as the gunships rolled in, destroying the enemy unit. The door guns fell silent and the nose of the chopper came up as they began a quick climb to fifteen hundred feet.

Gerber twisted around and sat up. He looked at Braver's body, at the bullet hole in the center of his back and the second one in his shoulder. He stared at the blood soaking the man's uniform and smelled the odor of hot copper as it filled the interior of the chopper, overwhelming the smell of JP-4, sweat and humidity. Scowling, he shook his head. "Damn!"

16

Gerber finally moved from his position behind the pilots' seats and sat down next to Fetterman who was staring at the body of Braver. "Poor kid," the master sergeant muttered, raising his voice so he could be heard over the roar of the turbine.

"Poor dumb kid," said Kepler.

Gerber looked at the intelligence NCO. "You still have ammo for that silenced pistol of yours?"

Kepler glanced at the captain. "Plenty of ammo for it. Magazine is fully loaded."

"Give it to me."

Fetterman looked at Gerber. He had a hard set to his eyes, and his lips were compressed into a thin line. "Captain, this might not be a good idea."

"That was once too often," said Gerber.

"What's going on?" asked Kepler.

Gerber stared at him. "We were set up. Maxwell set us up. I don't know why, but it's not going to happen again."

"How?"

"I don't know, but think about it. The enemy slipped into the jungle right behind us. Most of them were gone from the camp before we even arrived and then they circled around, taking positions behind us. Only way they could do that was if they knew we were there."

"Then why didn't they just slip closer and attack us?" asked Kepler.

"Good question. Obviously they were waiting for us to shoot their general. I don't know why they wanted him dead, but they were there to prevent us from getting away."

Kepler sat there grim-faced. He looked at the body lying on the floor of the cargo compartment, blood beginning to pool under it. Slowly he reached under his jungle jacket and extracted the pistol. But he didn't hand it over. "I'd be happy to take care of the problem, Captain."

"Thank you, Derek, but no. This is something I want to do myself."

"Sir," said Fetterman.

"Go with me, Tony." said Gerber. "Derek, I'll want you and Tyson to see about getting Braver home."

"Yes, sir."

Fetterman leaned closer to Gerber. "You can't just go in there with your pistol blazing."

"Thank you for the advice, Master Sergeant."

"Then you have a plan?"

"Yes, I've got a plan."

The crew chief looked around from his well and shouted, "You want to hit graves registration first or land at Hotel Three?"

"I want to land at the SOG pad," answered Gerber.

The crew chief was silent for a moment, then yelled, "We're about five minutes out."

Kepler surrendered the pistol. It was a small-caliber weapon with a long silencer fastened to its barrel. Gerber made sure the safety was set, then tucked it away. Sitting back, he tried to think of all the times Maxwell had fucked them over. Times he hadn't given them all the information available, or had thought they would be killed and hadn't bothered to arrange for transport, or hadn't told them the whole plan. Each time had angered Gerber, but this time he and his men had been sent out to be sacrificed for something that no one could understand. He felt pure rage wash over him, and in his mind he could see himself pumping bullets into Maxwell's smiling face.

"How are we going to do this?" asked Fetterman.

Gerber turned and studied the master sergeant. "I haven't thought about it."

"Then let's land and get cleaned up. Wash up and then head over to MACV."

"No," said Gerber. "I don't want to delay. I want to get this over as quickly as possible. I don't want to think about it any longer than I have to."

They began the descent toward the SOG pad. Tan Son Nhut spread out in front of them. They landed quickly in a swirling cloud of blowing dust and scraps of paper.

Gerber hopped out, waited and watched as Kepler and Tyson pulled Braver's body from the aircraft and placed it on the ground. With Fetterman and Thai, they pulled out the rest of their equipment. As soon as they had everything clear, the chopper picked up to a hover, turned and took off. In seconds the noise was gone and the dust settled. They were left in the blazing tropical sun with only the distant hum of the city and the sound of jet engines being revved at the far end of the airfield.

"Captain?" asked Kepler.

"Use a poncho liner and cover him."

Fetterman had disappeared inside the building and returned with a damp towel. He tossed it to Gerber, who snagged it with one hand and used it to wipe his face. He then threw it back at the master sergeant.

"Captain," said Tyson, "I'm not sure what I'm supposed to do now."

"Stay with Sergeant Kepler and we'll think of something when we get back."

"Yes, sir."

"Captain," said Fetterman, "I've got the keys to a jeep if you're ready."

Gerber looked at the body, now covered with the camouflage pattern of a poncho liner, a green beret lying on the chest. He then looked up at Kepler, who nodded once. "Get even for us."

"That I'll do." He followed Fetterman around to the jeep and climbed into the passenger side. "I'm set."

"You're sure about this?"

"Positive."

MORROW SAT AT HER DESK and tried to work her way through a pile of papers, but she couldn't concentrate. She was no longer interested in the various hows and whys of the Vietnam War. Stories of rocket and mortar attacks were of no interest to her. It was like the stories of fires in the World. Unless it was your house that burned down, or someone you knew, the story was of no real significance. All it did was fill airtime, sometimes providing good pictures, and that was all.

Hodges appeared at her desk and glanced at her. He looked around the room, and when he saw Danforth wasn't near, he said, "I think we've got a major problem."

Morrow, happy with the diversion, rocked back in her chair and laced her fingers behind her head. "What's your problem?"

Hodges ran a hand through his greasy black hair and perched himself on the edge of Morrow's desk. "Danforth. The little creep isn't going to work out."

"Now how could you know that? Already."

"Been on the phone all morning. All kinds of people calling to complain about him. Civilians and military. Most of them have the same message—don't send him over because we won't talk to him."

"So?"

"I've got to send him home, or move him somewhere else. Maybe up to Da Nang. Point is, he's of no use to me here, where I could use the help."

"Why tell me this?" asked Morrow.

Hodges refused to look at her. "We run hot and cold here. Some days there's more work than a staff twice as large as ours can handle. The next, we could get by on half. When we're busy, I need people I can trust, people who can do the job and who haven't alienated everyone over at MACV."

"There's always the embassy."

"Nope. He's pissed some of them off, too." Hodges finally looked up at her. "I sent him around with you to learn the ropes."

"He wasn't interested in learning them," said Morrow. "He already had his own ideas."

Hodges shrugged. "Doesn't really matter. I knew he wouldn't make a good reporter when he arrived. He already knew the answers before he asked the questions."

Morrow took a deep breath. "This leading where I think it is?"

"How badly did you want to go home?"

She shifted around and scratched her head. "I don't know. Things have stagnated here. It's always the same, day in and day out. Oh, the war continues, but you can only look at so many bodies before it begins to get to you. For a while you're immunized against it, hardened by it, but finally you can't take it anymore and have to get out.''

"Would a month's vacation work as well as a new assignment at home?''

Morrow took a deep breath. "I don't—''

"Paid for by us, of course. A nice free vacation anywhere in the world.''

Morrow rubbed a hand over her face and then through her hair. "Might work just fine.''

"I've got to get rid of Danforth. I thought you could break him in to take over for you. I thought he'd be your replacement, but he's just not going to work.''

"I'm stuck here.''

Hodges shook his head. "No, not if you really feel the need for time to yourself.''

"Okay," she said. "Get rid of Danforth and you can count on me, though it's not fair.''

"What's not fair?''

"I get the shitty jobs, do well at them and my reward is to get more of the same because I can do it. I screw it up and I get to try something else. Something better.''

"May not be fair, but it's the way things are. Sorry about it. Maybe I can squeeze some more money out of them for you. A little raise to make things a little fairer.''

She was about to tell him not to bother, but then said nothing. Why shouldn't she take more money if they wanted to give it to her?

"And Danforth?" she asked.

"I'm putting his ass on an airplane this afternoon, either for Da Nang or San Francisco. One way or the other, he's out of here today.''

"Hardly seems fair.''

"But it's the way things are." Hodges stood and turned to face her. "Thanks for not making this any harder than it had to be. I really didn't want to ask you to stay."

She grinned. "It's nice to be needed."

"Even here?" asked Hodges.

"Even here."

AT MAXWELL'S DOOR Fetterman caught Gerber by the shoulder and stopped him. "You're not going to just burst in and shoot him, are you?"

Gerber touched the grip of the pistol that was still stuck in the waistband of his fatigues. "No. I probably should, but I'm not going to."

"Because there's the possibility he isn't the leak," said Fetterman.

"Though it's more likely that he *is*."

"Talk first," said Fetterman.

Gerber glanced at the master sergeant but didn't say a word about his tone of voice. They'd been comrades too long for that. They'd been friends too long.

Without another word, Gerber touched the knob and threw open the door. He centered himself in the doorway and stared at Maxwell.

The CIA man jumped at the sudden noise. He whirled, his hand reaching for his pistol, which was hidden in the middle drawer of his desk. Then, when he recognized Gerber, he relaxed. "Thank God."

"What?"

Maxwell took a deep breath. "I spent all night over at SOG trying to recall you. The mission was compromised."

Gerber moved into the office, looked around as if searching for an ambush, then dropped into the visitor's chair. "Tell us about it, Jerry."

"Somehow word of it leaked. I was afraid you'd been compromised. I ordered the radio watch to alert you."

"Never got the message, Jerry," said Gerber.

"But you got out."

Fetterman entered finally and closed the door behind him, locking it. He grinned at Maxwell, then nodded at Gerber.

"What's all this?" asked Maxwell.

"We were set up, Jerry," said Gerber. "Set up to be killed."

"Not by me," said Maxwell, his voice rising. "When I found out I tried to recall you."

"The enemy knew we were there and what we were going to do."

"You can't know that," said Maxwell.

Gerber looked at Fetterman. "An interesting statement. We can't know that. What's that mean, Jerry? The plan was secret so we can't know that we were set up?"

"I mean," said Maxwell, speaking quickly, "that you'd have had to talk to the Cambodians to know that."

"What's to say we didn't."

"Let's stop playing games," said Maxwell. He twisted around in his chair and moved it back so that he could yank open the desk drawer if he felt the need.

"Good idea," said Gerber. "I have to tell you that I'm tired of all this. You send us out and the next thing we know our line of retreat is covered by a hundred enemy soldiers. But they don't attack us. They wait. Why's that?"

"I don't know," said Maxwell.

Gerber looked at Fetterman, who shrugged. "I don't think I believe him, sir."

"Neither do I."

"Tell us what's going on, Jerry."

Maxwell shrugged and outlined part of the plan, going over it in detail. He told them that their job had been a simple matter of eliminating a military officer who was assisting the North Vietnamese. "That's all," he said, "just as I told you before."

Gerber reached under his jacket and took out the silenced pistol.

"Oh, come on," said Maxwell, his voice tight. "You can't be serious."

"Why not? You set us up and we shoot our way clear. You have to expect this."

"But it wasn't me," said Maxwell. "I even had aviation assets standing by for a pickup."

"He's got a point there, Captain."

"A good cover," said Gerber. "For the moment I'll accept that. Now, who set us up?"

"No one," said Maxwell.

"Someone did, Jerry. We know it. The evidence is all there."

"It'll never stand up in court."

"That's what the guilty always say," Gerber growled. "Do you think because we can't prove it in court that it somehow doesn't count? Do you think that if I shoot you now, because I can't prove it in court, that you won't be dead?"

"Come on, Mack, we've known each other too long for this."

"I'll give you that, Jerry. Now, why shouldn't I just put a couple of bullets into your head?"

Maxwell relaxed slightly. He started to grin, stopped himself and said, "If you were really going to kill me, you'd have done it already. That means you're not as sure of yourself as you make out to be."

"Don't press your luck."

"Okay," said Maxwell, holding up his hands. "You want the truth? Call SOG and see if I wasn't there all night trying to get you out of the field. Just check that out, and if I'm lying, you can shoot me right between the eyes.''

Gerber looked at the silenced weapon in his hand, the barrel pointed at Maxwell. He turned it so that it was pointed at the floor. ''We were set up.''

''Okay,'' said Maxwell, nodding slowly, ''I believe you. But it wasn't me.''

''Someone did it,'' said Gerber.

''I doubt you were set up,'' said Maxwell, relaxing visibly. ''But someone could have been talking out of school. I can look into that.''

''No,'' said Gerber. ''I want a name. Now.''

''I can't give you a name now. I don't know who talked. Let me say this, I suspect it was one of our allies. We had to coordinate this operation with the South Vietnamese.''

''Won't wash,'' said Gerber. ''The South Vietnamese have taken the blame for all the problems, leaks and fucked-up missions for too long. Sure, it wasn't your fault, Jerry. It was some unnamed South Vietnamese officer.''

''I can look into it,'' said Maxwell. ''Ask questions. See how they found out about your mission.''

Gerber suddenly felt tired. Nothing else. Just tired. Tired of the whole mess and tired of working with people with disposable honor, people who valued honor only when it was convenient. He stood suddenly. ''Tony, let's get out of here.''

''Yes, sir.''

Maxwell stood up, too. ''I'll let you know what I find out.''

Gerber stared at him. ''Don't bother. I'm sure it will be as useless as anything else you tell us.''

''Mack,'' he said.

Gerber ignored him and walked to the door. Fetterman unlocked it and they stepped out.

''I think you handled that well, sir,'' said Fetterman. ''It'd do no good to kill him.''

Gerber nodded. "Then why don't I feel better about it?"

As soon as Gerber was gone, Maxwell felt as if he had just received a reprieve and then a pardon from the governor. He'd been within sight of his sudden demise and had gotten out of it. Gotten away with it. He fell back into his chair and took a deep breath, exhaling slowly. Sweat trickled down his face and his sides. He was cold and clammy, but he was breathing easier. Gerber and Fetterman had been right about him, but he had talked his way out of it. Going to SOG had been the best thing he could have done. By doing that he had covered the CIA role in the mission. With the failure, Margarite might be realled and given a mission. She would be better at her new assignment. Maybe he wouldn't have to see her again.

Finally he sat up and looked at the papers on his desk. Slowly everything came into focus. He picked up one of the files, then dropped it. He sat there for a moment, trying to calm down. When his breathing slowed and his heart stopped hammering, he glanced at his watch and gathered up his papers. It was time to head upstairs and brief General Hansen about the ongoing mission.

He walked out the door, locked it and headed for the stairs to the first floor. When he got to Hansen's office, the others were already there, waiting for him. The exception was General Hansen.

As soon as Maxwell sat down, an aide knocked on the door and it opened. Hansen swept in, and as the men moved to stand, he waved. "Remain seated." Hansen took up his position at the head of the table, opened his leather folder, then looked at Maxwell. "This is your meeting. Let's go."

"I have only preliminary results of the mission," he said. "The target wasn't assassinated as planned, but the mission created enough trouble for him and enough of his men were killed so that he's no longer a threat."

Hansen nodded and made a note. "Please clarify."

"Our major concern, General, was that this man, Samphan, was in the pocket of the North Vietnamese. That was the purpose of the mission into Cambodia. Break his power there by assassinating him."

"And that mission failed."

Maxwell shrugged. "He wasn't killed, but the latest information we have, and this is just under an hour old is that his men have all slipped away. He's a general without an army."

"There are others," said Hansen.

"Yes, General, and other teams have been dispatched to take care of them. The results will be trickling in for the next few days."

Hansen sat there for a moment, his eyes on the CIA man. He shook his head finally. "No. Let's cut this thing off now. Recall all the teams."

"General," said Maxwell.

"No," said Hansen. "I want no more discussion on this. All teams are to be recalled. If we feel the need to attack some of these camps to kill the officers, we'll use the Air Force. It's safer for our men that way. It's the way it should have been done in the first place."

"We'll kill friendlies as well as enemies," said Maxwell.

"That point might be debatable, but I don't feel the need to debate it. Cancel the missions."

Maxwell shrugged. "Yes, sir." He realized that Gerber and Fetterman wouldn't be thrilled with this new information, but there was now someone else to blame—General Hansen and his staff.

"If there's nothing else," said Hansen.

Maxwell shrugged.

"Then we're adjourned."

GERBER HAD BEEN THINKING about taking Morrow to dinner, if she would get rid of Danforth. He had been thinking

about staying in his room and drinking himself uncon-
scious. He had been thinking about a number of things.
Morrow changed all that when she dropped in on him.

When Gerber opened the door, she was wearing a short
skirt and a red blouse. Her hair seemed to glow. She grinned
at him and asked, "Can I come in?"

Gerber nodded. "Sure. You want a drink?"

"Beam's, if you've got it."

Gerber laughed. "It's the only thing I've got. Say, that
Danforth clown isn't with you, is he? He's not hiding in the
hall, is he?"

Now she laughed. "Danforth's gone. On his way to Da
Nang. He alienated everyone."

Gerber opened his wardrobe and took out the bottle of
Beam's. He gave it to Morrow, and she took it into the bath-
room to pour herself a drink. When she reappeared, she said,
"I'm going home."

"Oh?" said Gerber.

"That's it. Oh?"

Gerber shrugged. "I thought we'd talked this out a couple of days ago."

"Not to my satisfaction."

"Okay," said Gerber. "How's this? Don't go."

"Why shouldn't I?"

Gerber knew there was no way around it this time. She was
going to press on until he told her exactly what she wanted
to hear. The thing was, he wanted to tell her so that she'd stay.
In the field, as the enemy had maneuvered around him, he
had realized that his only regret was that he hadn't told Morrow how he felt. He'd kept it bottled up inside. Now he
wanted her to know.

He stared into her eyes and told her exactly why he didn't
want her to go. When he was done, she nodded. "I guess I
don't need the Beam's now."

EPILOGUE

PHUM CHRES CAMBODIA

General Kong Samphan sat in the nearly deserted camp in what the Americans called the Parrot's Beak and wondered what had happened. Once the camp had been filled with his soldiers. Men who served him and who would serve the North Vietnamese. Now there were only a few soldiers. Men who had been too sick, too poorly trained or who had duties other than combat and had remained behind. The rest of the men were gone.

Samphan looked around his tiny headquarters, at the homemade table, the four rough chairs and the small field desk. And the picture of the blond woman with the big breasts. It was almost all that remained of his command. The headquarters hut, the other buildings around it and twelve or thirteen men. The other men and their weapons and equipment were gone.

And he had no idea what had happened. Firing in the jungle around them, then firing farther away, and then nothing. His men attacking, or being attacked, heavy shooting, and then ominous silence.

A noise outside drew his attention, and Samphan stood and walked to the door. Looking out, he watched the approach of a North Vietnamese squad. They were a tired-looking group, their green uniforms sweat-stained and dirty. All wore packs and carried canteens and AKs. One of them had a pistol.

Samphan stepped from his headquarters hut and approached the North Vietnamese. He didn't recognize any of them. They weren't the same men who had visited him before.

"Welcome," called Samphan, holding a hand up in greeting.

The NVA officer halted his men with a wave of the hand. They spread out and formed a rough circle, as if they were alone in the jungle. The officer moved forward. "We found the remains of your men. Dead in the jungle. Many of them lost their weapons. Some threw them away."

"My men wouldn't throw away their guns."

"No matter. We found the remains of the battle scattered throughout the jungle from here to the South Vietnamese border. There were many who might have lived if their friends hadn't abandoned them."

"Sometimes it's necessary in battle to leave the injured until they can be cared for later," said Samphan.

"Sometimes it's necessary to leave them for good," agreed the NVA officer. He looked around the camp. "How many men are left with you here, General?"

"Enough."

"Are you sure?" said the NVA officer.

"Please," said Samphan, ignoring the question, "it's too hot and uncomfortable to talk out here. Make my quarters your home."

The NVA officer stepped up the notched log, looked at the rough table and chairs and then sat down so that his back was to neither the door nor the window.

"Would you care for a drink?" asked Samphan.

"Later. When our business is concluded."

Samphan sat down opposite the NVA officer. "Whom do I have the pleasure of addressing?"

"Names are unimportant. Only deeds."

"It makes for a more congenial atmosphere for our discussion if we trade names," said Samphan.

The officer ignored the statement. He leaned forward, elbows on the table, hands in plain sight. "All your men are dead, General."

"I know," said Samphan sadly. "They were out on maneuvers when they ran into the Americans. It's the only answer I can think of."

"The Americans sent an assassin to kill you," said the officer.

Samphan's eyes widened and the color drained from his face. "To kill me. Why?"

"Our sources don't know the reasons, only that men came to shoot you and that your men plundered into them, stopping them and saving your life."

"My brave soldiers," he said.

"But a general without an army isn't a general in anything but name."

"I shall raise a new army and train them better. They'll be good soldiers."

"And how will you equip these soldiers?" asked the NVA officer.

"As I have in the past. With help from my comrades in Vietnam and from the weapons and ammunition taken from the bodies of the dead enemy we leave on the field."

"A prospect that could take years," said the officer. He leaned back and dropped his left hand into his lap. "But now you could provide a lesson of greater value. One that could be accomplished today. Now."

Samphan leaned forward, eager to hear the plan. "How can I help?"

"By dying for your failure."

"What?"

"A general who allows his men to go out and die for him and doesn't die with them is nothing. He's a foolish, vain, useless man."

"I don't understand."

"And that's the problem," said the officer. He stared at Samphan, locking his eyes with those of the Cambodian general as he drew his pistol. He aimed it under the table and pulled the trigger once.

Samphan took the round in the belly. At first he felt nothing and wondered what had happened. But then the red-hot pain thrust into his stomach, radiating outward, down into his groin and up into his chest.

Now the officer lifted his hand above the table, aimed at a point between Samphan's eyes and fired again. A third, darkened eye appeared in his forehead as the back of his head blew off, splattering the blond's picture with blood and brain.

Samphan flipped over, taking the chair with him. He groaned once and his feet drummed on the floor. Blood bubbled from his mouth, staining the rough planking. The officer watched as he slowly died, and when the jerking movements of the feet stopped, the breathing halted and the heaving of the chest stilled, he spun and walked out of the hut.

The survivors of Samphan's army were gathered around. None of them had weapons. They were a motley crew, dirty, skinny, and one man without a left arm. It explained why they hadn't died with the others. They hadn't been fit enough to survive in the jungle, especially in a fight.

The officer was going to say something to them, but couldn't find the right words. He knew that once he left and they found the body of their general, they would drift away. Maybe not today or tomorrow, but soon, as the food and supplies ran out, they would go.

Without a word to them, he waved a hand and then walked down the notched log, past his men and toward the jungle. His men fell in behind him, two or three breaking off as a rear guard in case the Cambodians decided to get even.

As he entered the jungle, he knew that wouldn't happen, not with all their leaders dead or missing. The book had been closed on this one.

GLOSSARY

AC—Aircraft commander. The pilot in charge of the aircraft.

ADO—A-Detachment's area of operations.

AFVN—Armed Forces radio and television network in Vietnam. Army PFC Pat Sajak was probably the most memorable of AFVN's DJs with his loud and long "GOOOOOOOOOOOOOD MORNing, Vietnam!" The spinning wheel of fortune gives no clues about his whereabouts today.

AGGRESSOR FATIGUES—Black fatigues worn by the aggressors during war games in the World during training.

AIT—Advanced Individual Training. The school soldiers were sent to after basic.

AK-47—Assault rifle normally used by the North Vietnamese and the Vietcong.

ANGRY-109—AN-109, the radio used by the Special Forces for long-range communications.

AN/PRR9 and AN/PRT4—Intrasquad radio receiver and transmitter used for short-range communications under a mile.

AO—Area of Operations

AO DAI—Long dresslike garment, split up the sides and worn over pants.

AP—Air Police. The old designation for the guards on Air Force bases. Now referred to as security police.

AP ROUNDS—Armor-piercing ammunition.

ARVN—Army of the Republic of Vietnam. A South Vietnamese soldier. Also known as Marvin Arvin.

ASA—Army Security Agency.

ASH AND TRASH—Refers to helicopter support missions that didn't involve a direct combat role. They hauled supplies, equipment, mail and all sorts of ash and trash.

AST—Control officer between the men in isolation and the outside world. He is responsible for taking care of all problems.

AUTOVON—Army phone system that allows soldiers on one base to call another base, bypassing the civilian phone system.

BDA—Bomb Damage Assessment. Official report on how well a bombing mission went.

BIG RED ONE—Nickname of the First Infantry Division. It is derived from the shoulder patch, a big, red numeral one.

BISCUIT—C-rations.

BODY COUNT—Number of enemy killed, wounded or captured during an operation. Used by Saigon and

Washington as a means of measuring progress of the war.

BOOM BOOM—Term used by Vietnamese prostitutes in selling their product.

BOONDOGGLE—Any military operation that hasn't been completely thought out. An operation that is ridiculous.

BOONIE HATS—Soft cap worn by a grunt in the field when not wearing his steel pot.

BROWNING M-2—Fifty-caliber machine gun manufactured by Browning.

BROWNING M-35—The 9 mm automatic pistol that became the favorite of the Special Forces.

BUSHMASTER—Jungle warfare expert or soldier skilled in jungle navigation. Also a large deadly snake not common to Vietnam but mighty tasty.

C AND C—Command and Control aircraft that circled overhead to direct combined air and ground operations.

CAO BOI—A cowboy. Refers to criminals of Saigon who rode motorcycles.

CAR-15—Short barreled version of the M-16 with telescoping stock.

CARIBOU—Cargo transport plane.

CHECKRIDE—Flight in which one pilot checks the proficiency of another. It can be an informal review of the various techniques or a very formal test of a pilot's knowledge.

CHINOOK—Army Aviation twin-engine helicopter. A CH-47. Also known as a shit hook.

CHOCK—Refers to the number of the aircraft in a flight. Chock Three is the third. Chock Six is the sixth.

CLAYMORE—Antipersonnel mine that fires seven hundred and fifty steel balls with a lethal range of fifty meters.

CLOSE AIR SUPPORT—Use of airplanes and helicopters to fire on enemy units near friendlies.

CO CONG—Female Vietcong.

COLT—Soviet-built small transport plane. The NATO code names for Soviet and Warsaw Pact transports begin with the letter *C*.

COMSEC—Communications security.

CONEX—Steel container about ten feet high, ten feet deep and ten feet long used to haul equipment and supplies.

CS—Refers to a tear gas type chemical used in Vietnam. Actually it was a fine powder that could lie undisturbed for weeks until stirred up by men walking through it or by the rotor wash of landing helicopters.

DAC CONG—Enemy sappers who attacked in the front ranks to blow up the wire so that the infantry could assault a camp.

DAI UY—Vietnamese army rank equivalent to captain.

DEROS—Date Estimated Return from Overseas Service.

DIRNSA—Director, National Security Agency.

E AND E—Escape and Evasion.

FEET WET—Term used by pilots to describe flight over water.

FIELD GRADE—Refers to officers above the rank of captain but under brigadier general. In other words, majors, lieutenant colonels and colonels.

FIRECRACKER—Special artillery shell that explodes into a number of small bomblets that detonate later. The artillery version of the cluster bomb. A secret weapon employed tactically for the first time at Khe Sanh.

FIREFLY—Helicopter with a battery of bright lights mounted in or on it. The aircraft is designed to draw enemy fire at night so that gunships orbiting close by can attack the target.

FIRST SHIRT—Military term referring to a first sergeant.

FIVE—Radio call sign for the executive officer of a unit.

FNG—Fucking New Guy.

FOB—Forward Operating Base.

FOX MIKE—FM radio.

FREEDOM BIRD—Name given to any aircraft that took troops out of Vietnam. Usually referred to the commercial jet flights that took men back to the World.

GUARD THE RADIO—Term that means standing by in the commo bunker and listening for messages.

GUNSHIP—Armed helicopter or cargo plane that carries weapons instead of cargo.

HE—High explosive ammunition.

HOOTCH—Almost any shelter, from temporary to long-term.

HORN—Term that referred to a specific kind of radio operations that used satellites to rebroadcast messages.

HORSE—See *Biscuit*.

HOTEL THREE—Helicopter landing area at Saigon's Tan Son Nhut Airport.

HUEY—UH-1 helicopter.

HUMINT—Human intelligence resource.

ICS—Official name for the intercom system in an aircraft.

IN-COUNTRY—Term used to refer to American troops operating in South Vietnam. They were all in-country.

INTELLIGENCE—Any information about enemy operations that would be useful in planning a mission.

JP-4—Enhanced kerosene fuel burned in jets and jet turbine helicoprters.

KIA—Killed in Action. (Since the U.S. wasn't engaged in a declared war, the use of the term KIA wasn't authorized. KIA came to mean enemy dead. Americans were KHA or Killed in Hostile Action.)

KLICK—A thousand meters. A kilometer.

LIMA LIMA—Land Line. Refers to telephone communications between two points on the ground.

LLDB—Luc Luong Dac Biet. South Vietnamese Special Forces. Sometimes referred to as the Look Long, Duck Back.

LP—Listening Post. A position outside the perimeter manned by a couple of people to give advance warning of enemy activity.

LRRP—Long-Range Reconnaissance Patrol.

LSA—Lubricant used by soldiers on their weapons to ensure they would continue to operate properly.

LZ—Landing Zone.

M-3—Also known as a grease gun. A .45-caliber submachine gun that was favored in World War II by GIs. Its slow rate of fire meant the barrel didn't rise. As well, the user didn't burn through his ammo as fast as he did with some of his other weapons.

M-14—Standard rifle of the U.S., eventually replaced by the M-16. It fires the standard NATO round—7.62 mm.

M-16—Became the standard infantry weapon of the Vietnam War. It fires 5.56 mm ammunition.

M-79—Short-barreled, shoulder-fired weapon that fires a 40 mm grenade. These can be high explosives, white phosphorus or canister.

M-113—Numerical designation of an armored personnel carrier.

MACV—Military Assistance Command, Vietnam, replaced MAAG in 1964.

MATCU—Marine Air Traffic Control Unit.

MEDEVAC—Dust-Off. Helicopter used to take wounded to medical facilities.

MI—Military Intelligence.

MIA—Missing In Action.

MONOPOLY MONEY—Term used by servicemen in Vietnam to describe the MPC handed out in lieu of regular U.S. currency.

MOS—Military Occupation Specialty.

MPC—Military Payment Certificate. Used by military instead of real cash.

NCO—Noncommissioned Officer. A noncom. A sergeant.

NCOIC—NCO In Charge. The senior NCO in a unit, detachment or patrol.

NDB—Nondirectional beacon. A radio beacon that can be used for homing.

NEXT—The man who said he was the next to be rotated home. See *Short.*

NINETEEN—Average age of the combat soldier in Vietnam, as opposed to twenty-six in World War II.

NVA—North Vietnamese Army. Also used to designate a soldier from North Vietnam.

ONTOS—Marine weapon that consists of six 106 mm recoilless rifles mounted on a tracked vehicle.

ORDER OF BATTLE—A listing of the available units to be used during a battle. Not necessarily a list of how or when the units will be used, but a description of who and what could be used.

P (PIASTER)—Basic monetary unit in South Vietnam worth slightly less than a penny.

P-38—Small, folding can opener made of sheet metal issued with C-rations.

PETER PILOT—Copilot in a helicopter.

PLF—Parachute Landing Fall. The roll used by parachutists on landing.

POL—Petroleum, Oil and Lubricants. The refueling point on many military bases.

POW—Prisoner Of War.

PRC-10—Portable radio.

PRC-25—Lighter portable radio that replaced the PRC-10.

PULL PITCH—Term used by helicopter pilots that means they are going to take off.

PUNJI STAKE—Sharpened bamboo hidden to penetrate the foot. Sometimes dipped in feces.

REDLEGS—Term that refers to artillerymen. It derives from the old Army where artillerymen wore red stripes on the legs of their uniforms.

RINGKNOCKER—Graduate of a military academy. Refers to the ring worn by all graduates.

RLO—Real Live Officer. A term used by warrant officers to refer to commissioned officers.

RON—Remain Over Night. Term used by flight crews to indicate a flight that would last longer than a day.

RPD—Soviet 7.62 mm light machine gun.

RTO—Radio Telephone Operator. The radioman of a unit.

RUFF-PUFFS—Term applied to RF-PFs, the regional and popular forces. Militia drawn from the local population.

S-3—Company-level operations officer. Same as the G-3 on a general's staff.

SA-2—Surface-to-air missile fired from a fixed site. Radar-guided, it's nearly thirty-five feet long.

SA-7—Surface-to-air missile that is shoulder-fired and has infrared homing.

SACSA—Special Assistant for Counterinsurgency and Special Activities.

SAFE AREA—Selected Area for Evasion. It doesn't mean the area is safe from the enemy, only that the terrain, location or local population make the area a good place for escape and evasion.

SAM TWO—Refers to the SA-2 Guideline.

SAR—Search And Rescue. SAR forces were the people involved in search-and-rescue missions.

SECDEF—Secretary of Defense.

SFer—A Special Forces soldier.

SHORT-TIME—GI term for a quickie.

SHORT-TIMER—Person who had been in Vietnam for nearly a year and who would be rotated back to the

World soon. When the DEROS (Date of Estimated Return from Overseas Service) was the shortest in the unit, the person was said to be next.

SINGLE-DIGIT MIDGET—Soldier with fewer than ten days left in-country.

SIX—Radio call sign for the unit commander.

SKATE—Goldbricking.

SKS—Soviet carbine.

SMG—Submachine gun.

SOG—Studies & Observations Group. Cover name for MACV clandestine operations.

SOI—Signal Operating Instructions. The booklet that contained the call signs and radio frequencies of the units in Vietnam.

SOP—Standard Operating Procedure.

SPIKE TEAM—Special Forces team made up for a direct-action mission.

STEEL POT—Standard U.S. Army helmet. The steel pot was the outer metal cover.

TAOR—Tactical Area of Operational Responsibility.

TEAM UNIFORM OR COMPANY UNIFORM—UHF radio frequency on which the team or company communicates. Frequencies were changed periodically in an attempt to confuse the enemy.

THE WORLD—The United States.

THREE—Radio call sign of the operations officer.

THREE CORPS—Military area around Saigon. Vietnam was divided into four corps areas.

TOC—Tactical Operations Center.

TO&E—Table of Organization and Equipment. A detailed listing of all the men and equipment assigned to a unit.

TOT—Time Over Target. Refers to the time the aircraft is supposed to be over the drop zone with parachutists, or the target if the plane is a bomber.

TRIPLE A—Anti-aircraft Artillery or AAA. Anything used to shoot at airplanes and helicopters.

TWO—Radio call sign of the intelligence officer.

UMZ—Ultramilitarized Zone. Name GIs gave to the DMZ (Demilitarized Zone).

UNIFORM—Refers to the UHF radio. Company Uniform would be the frequency assigned to that company.

URC-10—UHF emergency radio used by long range patrols.

USARV—United States Army, Vietnam.

VC—Vietcong, called Victor Charlie (phonetic alphabet) or just Charlie.

VIETCONG—Contraction of Vietnam Cong San (Vietnamese Communist).

VIETCONG SAN—Vietnamese Communists. A term in use since 1956.

WHITE MICE—South Vietnamese military police who wore white helmets.

WIA—Wounded In Action.

WILLIE PETE—WP, white phosphorus, called smoke rounds. Also used as antipersonnel weapons.

WOBBLY ONE—Refers to a W-1, the lowest of the warrant officer grades. Helicopter pilots who weren't commissioned started out as wobbly ones.

XM-21—Name given to the Army's sniper rifle. An M-14 mounted with a special ART scope.

XO—Executive officer of a unit.

ZAP—To ding, pop caps or shoot. To kill.

The past blew out in 2001.
Welcome to the future.

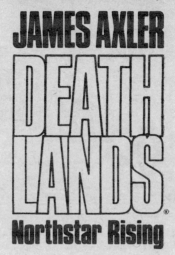

JAMES AXLER
DEATH LANDS®
Northstar Rising

A generation after a global nuclear war, Minnesota is a steamy tropical paradise of lush plants and horrifically mutated insects. In this jungle, Ryan Cawdor and his band of post-holocaust warriors uncover yet another freakish legacy of a world gone hideously wrong: Vikings.

ABLE TEAM

DICK STIVERS

Action writhes in the reader's own streets as Able Team's Carl ''Ironman'' Lyons, Pol Blancanales and Gadgets Schwarz make triple trouble in blazing war. Join Dick Stivers's Able Team—the country's finest tactical neutralization squad in an era of urban terror and unbridled crime.

''Able Team will go anywhere, do anything, in order to complete their mission. Plenty of action! Recommended!''
> —*West Coast Review of Books*

TAKE 'EM NOW

FOLDING SUNGLASSES
FROM GOLD EAGLE

Mean up your act with these tough, street-smart shades. Practical, too, because they fold 3 times into a handy, zip-up polyurethane pouch that fits neatly into your pocket. Rugged metal frame. Scratch-resistant acrylic lenses. Best of all, they can be yours for only $6.99.

MAIL YOUR ORDER TODAY.

Send your name, address, and zip code, along with a check or money order for just $6.99 + .75¢ for postage and handling (for a total of $7.74) payable to Gold Eagle Reader Service. (New York and Iowa residents please add applicable sales tax.)

Remove from pouch

unfold once

unfold twice

and they're ready to wear

Gold Eagle Reader Service
901 Fuhrmann Blvd.
P.O. Box 1396
Buffalo, N.Y. 14240-1396

GOLD EAGLE

GES-1A

Offer not available in Canada.

by GAR WILSON

The battle-hardened five-man commando unit known as Phoenix Force continues its onslaught against the hard realities of global terrorism in an endless crusade for freedom, justice and the rights of the individual. Schooled in guerrilla warfare, equipped with the latest in lethal weapons, Phoenix Force's adventures have made them a legend in their own time. Phoenix Force is the free world's foreign legion!

"Gar Wilson is excellent! Raw action attacks the reader on every page."
—Don Pendleton

Phoenix Force titles are available wherever paperbacks are sold.

PHOENIX FORCE

GOLD EAGLE

PF-1R

A different world—a different war

RED EQUINOX $3.95   ☐
Ryan Cawdor and his band of postnuclear survivors enter a
malfunctioning gateway and are transported to Moscow, where
Americans are hated with an almost religious fervor and blamed
for the destruction of the world.

DECTRA CHAIN $3.95   ☐
A gateway that is part of a rambling underwater complex brings
Ryan Cawdor and the group off the coast of what was once
Maine, where they are confronted with mutant creatures and
primitive inhabitants.

ICE & FIRE $3.95   ☐
A startling discovery changes the lives of Ryan Cawdor and his
band of postholocaust survivors when they encounter several
cryogenically preserved bodies.

Total Amount	$ _____
Plus 75¢ Postage	.75
Payment enclosed	$ _____

Please send a check or money order payable to Gold Eagle Books.

In the U.S.	In Canada
Gold Eagle Books	Gold Eagle Books
901 Fuhrmann Blvd.	P.O. Box 609
Box 1325	Fort Erie, Ontario
Buffalo, NY 14269-1325	L2A 5X3

Please Print

Name: _____

Address: _____

City: _____

State/Prov: _____

Zip/Postal Code: _____

GOLD
EAGLE

DL-B